A Case of Crime

A Beth Wade-Beechly mystery

D. M. Spinks

A Case of Crime

Copyright © 2015 Diane Spinks
All rights reserved. No part of this publication may be reproduced, stored in a retrieval system or transmitted in any form or by any means, electronic, mechanical, photocopying, recording or otherwise, without the prior written permission of the publisher.

The information, views, opinions and visuals expressed in this publication are solely those of the author(s) and do not reflect those of the publisher. The publisher disclaims any liabilities or responsibilities whatsoever for any damages, libel or liabilities arising directly or indirectly from the contents of this publication.

A copy of this publication can be found in the National Library of Australia.

ISBN: 978-1-742845-11-1 (pbk.)

Published by Book Pal
www. bookpal. com. au

Contents

PROLOGUE. ....

CHAPTER ONE. 1

CHAPTER TWO. 5

CHAPTER THREE. 14

CHAPTER FOUR. 26

CHAPTER FIVE. 35

CHAPTER SIX. 44

CHAPTER SEVEN. 60

CHAPTER EIGHT. 65

CHAPTER NINE. 80

CHAPTER TEN. 87

CHAPTER ELEVEN. 94

CHAPTER TWELVE. 104

CHAPTER THIRTEEN. 112

CHAPTER FOURTEEN. 119

CHAPTER FIFTEEN. 126

EPILOGUE. 134

PROLOGUE.

Elizabeth Wade-Beechly, Private Investigator - ...Elizabeth Wade-Beechly, Private Investigator. Beth held her business card in front of her as she sat at her office desk. The gold letters and matching border were neat, clear and organised reflecting nothing, she thought with a wry smile, of her own lifestyle. She couldn't help but think that the card should have more appropriately belonged to her big sister Sarah. Sarah always *was* the sensible one. Three years her senior and in a *permanent* state of order and control. In school she was top of her class, with awards and accolades in everything from creative writing as a child to Physics and Chemistry in her senior high school years, eventually going on to become one of the most successful students Cambridge University had ever opened its doors to. Beth was suspended in the second form for causing the explosion and resulting destruction of all three science labs "Ooh!", she remembered with a shudder and a shake of the head, "a nasty day, that. "

But, as with all of the adventures , or should one say misadventures she had caused and lived through, Beth had easily shrugged this one off with a mere "Hmm-oh well", and chalked it up to experience!

Sarah, she smiled to herself, poor old Sarah- honest, reliable, sensible; the picture of perfection really-which was why it came as such a shock to all (except Beth) when she was discreetly removed from the payroll of one of the most reputable banks in London. (A little matter of some forged signatures here and there).

It was no surprise to Beth. Surely, she had thought many a time, that bubbling just under the surface of all that perfection was a huge surge of 'naughtiness' just waiting to break through and unleash itself on an unsuspecting world. Unfortunately for Sarah, it had surfaced all at once! She was lucky (and constantly reminded of the fact) that their father had known a few of the 'right' people to keep the matter out of the courts. For the same reason-all those years ago-Beth had escaped unscathed through the science lab incident. She was very grateful-that was a fact-but seemed to have been thanking 'daddy dearest' for the twenty-odd years since.

Michael James Beechly the 2nd-like father like son. Beth smiled and shook her head-"only two words needed to describe the 'old man'-filthy rich. "But from what she could remember, that really seemed to be the *only* thing the two men had had in common. Beth's Grandfather, Michael James Beechly the 1st, or 'Beech 'as he had liked to be known, had founded 'BEECHLY INVESTMENTS AND FINANCIAL ADVISORY SERVICES, a hugely successful company with offices world-wide . Of course, this was only the main business interest. Beech had owned and directed companies and businesses in just about every field, in just about every corner of the globe. When he died, Michael junior had inherited the lot and, luckily for Beth and Sarah, this included not only the money, but also the 'friends' in some very high places-friends to know for when one found themselves in a 'slight spot of trouble'. And with Beth being Beth , this seemed to be quite a common occurrence.

Beth's mother, Maria was a confident and competent woman. The very fact that she had opted to keep her maiden name when she married Michael in 1958 told she was a woman of extreme independence. Maria and Michael had divorced when Beth was only five. After twelve years, two children, and countless 'ups and downs'(the last straw being Michael's affair with his nineteen year old secretary), they had decided to call it quits. That was thirty years ago and Maria had remained happily single ever since.

Both girls had always been closer to their mother and so, four years ago, when Sarah had felt the need to "....get away from it all....", Beth had decided to join her and together they went to live near their mother in California, where Maria now resided.

Beth had inherited Maria's dark hair which she wore in a neat and bouncy bob whereas Sarah was sandy blonde just like her father. Hence they were as different in appearance as they were in personality. But, despite the differences between them, they really were the very best of friends. Beth in fact, had felt that the forged signatures incident, or 'Sarah-Gate' as she liked to call it (much to Sarah's dismay) , had actually brought them closer together, and had been secretly rather impressed! In fact, it was Sarah's special 'skill' that had helped Beth out so many times in the past -*and* in the future . Long, long ago in the past and way way ahead in the future! For Beth was no ordinary Private investigator-Beth was simply no ordinary person. When she turned twenty one, her Grandmother had given her a *very* special gift. Not, as she had expected (and was kind of hoping for), the 'passed -down- through- generations' string of pearls, nor the beautifully engraved fob watch that Grandfather had owned since he was a boy, but something that shocked even Beth and of which her Grandmother alone knew the true secret.

Selina Beechly was a wondrous woman indeed, with a mind of her own which she used to full potential. She and Beech had travelled the world both together and separately and Selina had studied extensively, ancient cultures, religions and civilizations. Did this, Beth had often wondered, have a bearing on how she acquired her remarkable 'gift'? All Selina would ever say was that it was "....given to her in her sleep one night....by forces unknown...".

"Forces unknown!, " Beth said, shaking her head and placing the card back on the desk. " Slightly melodramatic, gran" her thoughts continued, " but I guess I can't begrudge you that-and goodness knows I put up with it on a daily basis working with Sarah!".

Selina had never explained it any other way and Beth being Beth had taken this as as good an explanation as any and had happily and gratefully accepted the remarkable gift being offered her. She had always said...'the importance of the power is not in its origin. . , but in how it is put to use'.

It was now the year 2000 and Beth was thirty four. Selina was alive and well and living with Maria in California-but at eighty five years of age, "just didn't have the strength "she would say, "to do the things I used to do, " giving Beth a wink to acknowledge their little secret. Although Selina was Michael's mother, she and Maria had always been more like mother and daughter. Maria's parents had died long before she and Michael married and to see them together, it was easy to forget that Maria was Selina's daughter in *law*.

Selina had not chosen Beth over Sarah as the recipient of her unique gift, but rather, had offered it to both her grand daughters. The elder had graciously denied the opportunity. The implications reached far beyond the scope of reality and order for Sarah, who was very comfortable in the lifestyle she had created for herself. Beth, on the contrary, had literally jumped at the chance! Selina was most definite however, about the one and only condition. "Elizabeth, my dear. ", Beth still remembered her words with love and admiration, "this is a most precious gift I am offering you. Please take it with my love, but use it only to help others-will you promise me that?" Beth didn't hesitate for a moment. She promised and meant it with everything she had. Her admiration for the older woman had doubled at hearing her words. Here stood a woman with the power to change lives-to alter the course of history; there were no limits to the power one could seize with such a gift! But not Grandma Selina-who had with one sentence, summed up exactly the woman she was.

And Beth's occupation was perfect. Time didn't stop crime. In every moment there would exist murder, theft, danger, excitement-and always someone unjustly accused of a crime they haven't committed. To Beth, being a Private Investigator was the most exciting thing in the world; and it was certainly a way of helping.

This meant she could live the life she loved as well as fulfill the promise she had made to her Grandmother. She felt happy and rather proud.

Putting her feet up on her desk and reclining in her plush office chair, she read her business card again, this time aloud..."Elizabeth Wade-Beechly-private investigator".

She laughed...then laughed again...'if only they knew the half of it....Elizabeth Wade-Beechly....- 'TIME-TRAVELLER'!!!

CHAPTER ONE.

"Wade-Beechly Investigations, may I help you? Oh, Mr. Edwards, yes, yes I know-I'm sorry-look Mr. Edwards, Ms. Wade-Beechly isn't in at the moment but I promise she'll contact you as soon as she....... yes I realize that and I'm really very sorry..... alright then Mr. Edwards, goodbye..... Beth, don't run back into that office-you come back here right now!" Sarah yelled with all the fierceness she could muster (which in Sarah's case wasn't a great deal). "You have to talk to him sometime and that's the fourth time this morning I've covered for you. "

"Sarah", Beth answered, knowing she had to face her, "the man's insane-you don't know him-he wants me to follow his dog. "

"His dog" replied Sarah sceptically.

"Yes I tell you Sarah, the man's quite mad. Look, apparently, since their divorce he and his ex-wife have shared custody of their poodle, Maxine and each Wednesday she takes her on an outing. Well he wants me to follow them to find out where they go so that the next day he can take little Maxine somewhere better-can you believe it?!"

"Yes, in this town I can . " replied Sarah nodding.

"So I take the case-what the heck I think to my-self-nice, easy, safe. But now I have Mr Edwards continuously ringing me up with suggestions on how I should ..."tackle the assignment"...;disguises I should wear, that sort of thing and get this- he even sends me the name of a good languages tutor so that I can get my accents right! Accents if you please! Honestly Sarah, the man's been reading way too many stories!"

"Then why continue the case?"

"Sarah, you know as well as I do that business hasn't been great since...well you know. "

"Since you lost Prince Aftul's 'Eye of Shavrah'. "

"Well...yes'" Beth answered sheepishly..."oh well it *was* only a piece of stone after all....", she half mumbled.

"Only a stone?-Beth, that 'stone' as you put it, happened to be one of the world's largest known rubies and now it's gone-vanished without a trace!"

"Yes alright, I get the point. No need to remind me. Anyway, I didn't lose it; you know as well as I do it was one of the Prince's own men who stole it- and so will the Prince know it !, once I prove it-then let's just see him try to apologize...'demon-woman' indeed!"

"Yes Beth. " said Sarah returning to her computer screen.

"Oh Sarah, don't forget we have a lunch date with Grandma Selina today-can't wait-maybe she has a new assignment for us!"

"For you, you mean" Sarah snapped. "You don't always have to include me you know. "

"Oh but Sarah, you've always helped me out so wonderfully. "

"Yes, and so illegally don't forget-forgery was exactly what got me into trouble in England, in *case* you'd forgotten. "

"Sarah"Beth said meaningfully, "you have a skill and sometimes I need you to use that skill to get me into places and situations in order to help innocent people. Anyway I'm usually in another century for heaven's sake-nobody's ever going to 'pin' anything on you. "

'Oh Beth, I do wish you wouldn't use such terms-you make me sound like a common criminal. I made a stupid mistake!"

Beth rolled her eyes. "Sarah the only mistake you ever made was getting caught. Anyway, I never liked you working for that firm-no future in it for you-too many family members to take all the good promotions." "Oh yes", Sarah replied sarcastically, "far better prospects for me here. Last job: forging documents for woman who travels through time. (That is, of course. when she's not following poodles)-how wonderful *that's* going to look on my resume." "But Sarah my darling", Beth replied smiling sweetly, "you'll never need a resume again-you can work for me forever!" "Hmm well go and do some work so that I still have a job to come to. "Sarah said sternly but with a hint of a smile. "Sarah", Beth said cheekily, "you always *were* my favourite sister." "Well I'd want to be seeing I'm you're *only* one. "

Beth ran for the safety of her office door as she saw Sarah reaching for a crumpled piece of paper. "Now let me get this typing done or we'll have more irate clients phoning us up!", Sarah yelled in fun, throwing the ball of paper at Beth. "And I won't speak to Mr. Edwards again!", she added as the door closed between them.

A few moments went by before Beth slowly opened the door again.

"Sarah", she said, more seriously than before, "you will help..... if I need you?"

"Oh yes Beth, you know I will. ", Sarah replied in the martyr-like tone for which she had become famous.

"Good!-and if you get caught I'll come and visit you in the 'can'!"

"Right! "This time Sarah jokingly picked up a glass paperweight and Beth was gone in a flash!

CHAPTER TWO.

Lunch was at 'Cafe good'-and as the name suggested-it really was! A cute and quirky place about five minutes walk from the office, it was Beth's favourite place to eat-not too big that it was impersonal-yet just big enough to feel anonymous if in that kind of mood. It had the look of the old Dutch 'brown' cafes of Amsterdam(but without the smoke-stained walls)and served up *the* best coffee in town . The music was always loud enough that you could carry on a private conversation at normal pitch-but not so loud that it ever became annoying. . and it *always* differed depending on the owner Beverly's mood. Today, the customers were being treated a mixed collection of classic jazz divas and bev could been seen dancing in the kitchen to Peggy Lee's 'fever'. Selina appeared to be enjoying it immensely , happily tapping her fingers to the beat as she held the menu out in front of her. She was immaculately dressed in a white blouse and lemon jacket. She wore a dark green string of beads to match her skirt and shoes and although she was 'loaded' Beth thought to herself, there wasn't a pretentious bone in this lady's body. Here was a woman whose wealth easily amounted to several million dollars, yet here she sat in a busy little vegetarian cafe wearing a string of plastic beads and looking like a million 'bucks'. She loved her dearly.

Beth glanced over at Sarah and couldn't help thinking how glad she was that they hadn't come yesterday. Bev had turned fifty and was well and truly having a Janis Joplin day . Sarah would not have coped with that at all. Grandma maybe-Sarah NO! She had taken after their father in the sense that she could never quite relax and would always see the glass half empty as opposed to half full. In their father it was boring, often even offensive but in Sarah it was amusing-she never meant any harm.

Suddenly, lost in her thoughts, she realized that Sarah was actually speaking to her. "Beth-Beth, stop daydreaming and tell me what tempeh is quickly, here comes Beverly!"

"Well then girls, are we ready to order? Nice to see you again Mrs. Beechly. "

"Lovely to see you again too Bev, but please, it's Selina. "

"Well after yesterday you're practically the same age", Beth said cheekily.

"Keep her in line will you Selina?", replied Bev, playfully kicking Beth's chair, "I do have the authority to throw the trouble-makers out you know!"

They all laughed including the two women at the next table who had overheard Beth's comment.

"Well, if these two haven't made up their minds, I certainly have. "

Bev wrote down Selina's order and turned to Beth. "Do I really have to ask?", she said smiling.

"No, the usual for me. "

"The blue cheese souffle followed by the biggest piece of chocolate mud cake I can find, right?"

"You know me too well", Beth said with a wink. "I promise you Bev, one day I *will* try something different!"

Beth's description of tempeh must have conjured up far from a delight in Sarah's mind...she opted for the French onion soup.

They talked and laughed as they enjoyed their first course. Even Sarah had managed to lighten up a little, throwing all caution to the wind and ordering dessert!

"I hope you're still hungry", laughed Bev as she handed Beth what looked more like two pieces of cake than one. "I don't know where you girls put it", said Selina watching Beth happily 'digging in'[1] whilst Sarah prodded her pecan pie cautiously with a fork.

It was a wonderful lunch and once again Beth was so full she felt ill-but of course it was worth it! "Now girls", Selina said, dabbing her mouth with her napkin and straightening herself up, "we have some work to do. "

Beth's eyes widened, Sarah cringed. It had been almost twelve months since Beth had 'travelled' and quite frankly she was becoming a little bored with day to day life and work in San Paledino. She wondered to where Grandma Selina would be guiding her this time. Her previous assignment in 1740 had been a huge success and Beth was more than ready to undertake whatever was asked of her -in whatever time or place. "I can see that you're rather anxious to hear what I have for you Beth, so I'll get straight to the point. "

Beth's mind raced, full to the brim with anticipated ideas of what was in store for her-France in the middle ages;the early colonial days of Australia;or would she be having to brush up on her hunting and gathering skills?! The possibilities were endless and the adrenalin made her heart beat faster and faster. She quickly took a sip of coffee to bring her back to reality. "Not so far back this time dear", continued Selina, "in fact, to a time and place very familiar to you. "

Beth frowned, questioningly and waited. "You're off to London in 1965." "Oh...I see!", she said smiling and sitting back in her chair.

London; 1965 - the exact city and year in which she was born. The idea of returning as an adult was a very exciting prospect indeed. But this was no pleasure trip-this was business and Beth knew it as her mind returned to the task at hand. "What's happened Grandma, what's it all about-and when do I leave?"

Beth was excited but Sarah looked concerned. Her 'lightness' had rapidly disappeared. "Aren't you forgetting something Beth?"

Beth looked puzzled(or pretended to be). "A little matter of a spoilt poodle?" "Oh. "

"Yes oh!", Sarah continued, "I can't keep covering for you forever you know. "

"Sarah, my wonderful and competent sister I'm sure you'll think of something!"

"Well I suppose I'll just have to won't I?", Sarah replied, pretending to hate the idea but secretly thriving on the responsibility. "And I suppose you'll be needing *my* services one way or another?"

"If you would be so kind, Sarah my dear. "

"Oh yes Grandma, " Sarah's voice softened, "you know I don't mind really. "

"Well then girls, if you're ready, I'll go and pay Beverly and I thought we might go to my apartment for coffee-and yes, Beth-we *do* have decaf, " she said with a smile.

Beth gave her that 'Grandma I wasn't going to ask that' look (even though she was). One caffeine hit per day was her limit-especially one of the Cafe good's brews! She had really enjoyed lunch but felt it was time to leave anyway-Bev had that Joplin look in her eyes again! "You *will* be ready to 'go' this afternoon won't you Beth?"

Beth was surprised and it showed. "Today?" she said, looking sheepishly over at Sarah. "Yes Beth, off you go-I'll somehow manage to keep the office in order."

"Wonderful, then it's settled-I'll call Rex and have him take us home;your mother is anxious to see you before she leaves for Rome." "Rome?", Sarah asked rolling her eyes, "why on earth is she going to Rome?"

"Oh a painting or sculpture course or something of the like. She promised your Aunt Dorothy she'd do the course with her-personally I think Dorothy has designs on the gentleman running the show. Somebody by the name of Antonio Simbrizzi-supposed to be world famous-never heard of the chap myself." "Designs!" said Beth, raising one eyebrow at Sarah with both trying extremely hard to suppress their laughter. "Well they certainly keep themselves busy, the old girls!"

Selina and Maria's apartment was in Regency Gardens, one of San Paledino's more prominent suburbs. Beth loved the area but it just felt too 'rich[1] for her. She much prefered her and Sarah's little apartment down in Hazelton Road-right in the middle of the city. (Even if it *was*"a little too close to the wrong side of the tracks "in Daddy's opinion).

Beth loved the 'bigness' of the city. . the hustle , the bustle. . she loved just to 'people-watch and more than anything she loved catching up with friends at 'Cafe good. '

On the way they had decided to drop Sarah off at Hazelton road so that she could ever so skillfully produce a 1965 driver's licence for Beth. She left them reluctantly agreeing but Beth and Selina knew that she couldn't wait to get inside and get started! "She loves it Gran, "Beth chuckled, waving from the car window. "She wasn't cut out to be law abiding, our Sarah!"Selina couldn't help but laugh agreeingly.

Rex (Selina's devoted driver of over thirty years) helped Selina from the car, despite her constant protests. "I can still manage on my own thankyou" she would say time after time.

"Yes ma'am", Rex would reply diligently, but this time with a slight smile at Beth's mimicking behind her grandmother's back.

"Beth my darling, how are you?!!", was the greeting they received on entering the apartment. "Hello Mother-you look sensational!"

She hugged her and immediately , Maria started to apologize.

"Darling I can't talk, Dorothy will be here at any moment and we have to go straight to the airport", she said. frantically checking things off a list she was holding. "Honestly, I can't understand where this new love of art has stemmed from but well, I suppose I might learn something-can't hurt. "

Maria was an extremely attractive woman of sixty. She looked wonderful for her age and was someone who believed in growing old gracefully . There was no mistaking Beth for her daughter. The same dark brown, almost mischievous eyes;that 'ready to take on the world' stance. Selina had gone to the kitchen to make the coffee. "I won't have time for one thanks Mum", Maria called down the hallway. "Dorothy won't wait for anything-you know what she's like- gold or silver, sweetheart?" She turned to Beth holding two fine chains to her neck. "Silver", Beth said smiling.

"Thankyou darling-knew I could count on you- Do I look alright?" "Mum, you look fantastic"Beth said, meaning every word.

Maria was wearing a Navy blue pant suit with a lilac blouse, the touch of silver setting the ensemble off perfectly.

Beth's concentration was broken by the honking of a car horn and a ...."Maria are you ready?", wafting or more like rapidly scaling up the front of the apartment block. "Oh Lord there she is now- better not keep her waiting!"

Maria gathered her cases and was in the elevator before Beth could even offer to help.

"Love you darling bye Mum I'll be back on the 10th tell Sarah I'll call her then . . and take care!!!", the last few words being muffled by the closing of the elevator doors.

Beth and Selina went to the front window to wave. Bustling Maria into the passenger seat of a hired black Mercedes, was Dorothy-bottle red hair and lavender scarves flying in the wind. Dorothy was Maria's older sister. Everyone knew she was seventy three but mentioning her age was a definite no no!. Maria had obviously told her sister that Beth was inside as Dorothy called "Hello dear!", and blew her a kiss. Beth smiled and waved and within a few moments she was back in the car and they were off and out of sight. "Phew, did all that just happen?"

"Yes, exhausting isn't it ?", Selina said placing a tray of two steaming cups and plate of homebaked apple tarts on the coffee table, "But one gets used to it", she sighed.

Three hours passed quickly as the two women chatted about some previous travel 'assignments' and the present day ones Beth had on her books back at the office. There was a buzz on the intercom. That'll be Sarah-I'll get it Gran." "It's only me. "

"Come on up, sis", replied Beth and waited to open the door. "Well, this is the best I could do at such short notice", said Sarah. knowing it was practically perfect and waiting for the praise to commence.

'Oh Sar's it's wonderful-thankyou!" , Beth said kissing her on the cheek.

"Yes my dear" agreed Selina, "you've outdone yourself this time. " Sarah sat down happily and helped herself to the one remaining apple tart.

"Wow my very own 1960's driver's licence-look Gran" said Beth excitedly, "Elizabeth Wade-Beechly;D. O. B:-1930!" "Yes. very well done indeed, our Sarah. " Selina said proudly.

Selina paused and took a deep breath . "Well my girls-I think it's time. Alright darling Beth, you know the procedure-and we'll expect to see you every few days. " Beth took Selina's hand as Sarah looked on. "Good luck, Beth", she whispered. "Thanks sis-I'll see you soon. "

Beth closed her eyes and faded slowly from their sight. And when she opened them again, was in a totally different place and time.

CHAPTER THREE.

Beth looked around, wide-eyed and took a long deep breath to absorb all that she saw.

"London, 1965", she said in almost a whisper and a broad smile appeared on her face. She had experienced so many 'times' but this felt different-special. She didn't know if it was the fact that this was the year and place in which she was born or whether it was just the whole fascination with the 60's that she had always had. Beth owned a huge 1960's record collection and had decorated most of the apartment in Hazelton Road with 50's and 60's memorabillia (much to Sarah's constant disapproval!) She could never quite decide what bothered her sister the most-the psychedelic linoleum topped coffee table in the living room or the autographed poster of Cilla Black in the lavetory.

She nodded to herself, "the poster I think", and with a chuckle, returned her thoughts to the moment.

She walked about half a block still reeling from the very fact that she was actually here and came across a paperstand. Picking up the first newspaper she came to, she looked straight at the date. "March 28, 1965" she said softly. not even realizing she was speaking aloud, "I wasn't even born." "Did you say something, Miss?" The man behind the counter was looking up at her.

"Er yes the weather going to be warm. "

"That'll make a change Miss, still been quite cool of late." "Yes, right then", Beth said placing the newspaper back on the counter, still momentarily lost in her own thoughts. "Goodbye then", she added. "Cheerio Miss-have a nice day. "

He was looking at her strangely as she walked away and she didn't blame him.

"Get your thoughts together old girl and let's get on with the task at hand-whatever that may be", she said to herself scoldingly.

But she barely had time to do so before the blare of a police siren startled her so much by it's closeness that it made her jump. She watched with great interest as two young police constables and what appeared to be a plain-clothed detective, hurried from the car and into a building not more than fifty metres from where she was standing. In an instant, and in true Beth Wade-Beechly fashion, she was running to join them at the scene.

Slowing down to within a few paces, she realized it was the store of 'Sutton's Fine Jewellery'. Gosh, thought Beth, what's happened here?Almost before the thought had left her head, and, in the manner she had inherited from her mother, she found herself marching straight for the doorway. She was so determined in her stride that she almost walked straight into the hand that was extending to stop her.

"Hold on there Miss, "said the bright but strong voice of a fresh-faced young constable, "Police business Miss-no one allowed in unless authorized. "

Beth smiled;this young man had been given a job to do and he intended to do it well. "Quite so, Constable you have your orders, I understand. "

She pulled from her pocket her identification and said very directly, looking straight into his eyes. "Elizabeth Wade-Beechly.. I'm here on authority from Scotland Yard. "

At seeing the surprise on his face, she quickly added "If you'd like to check Constable, you may do so by contacting Superintendent Phillip Burton who will, I am sure be more than happy to verify that authority. "

"N-no Ma'am", he replied standing to attention, "that won't be necessary Ma'am. "

"Thankyou Constable?"

"Oh, Lee Somersby Ma'am-Milton street. "

"Well thankyou P. C. Somersby", she said with a smile, "I shall let your superiors know of your efficiency in this matter. "

"Oh thankyou very much Ma'am, "he replied standing straightly.

Beth made her way into the store feeling a little guilty at having made P. C. Somersby so uncomfortable;he had seemed like a decent young chap, she thought, who really *was* only doing his job. The sound of the words 'Scotland Yard[1] must have sent him into a panic and it was obvious he was never going to check up on Beth's story and risk being in even more trouble than he thought he may have already been in. The truth *was* that Beth had used the first name that had come into her head for the non-existent Scotland Yard 'super'. In reality, Phillip

Burton was actually Beth's hair stylist , who would have passed out with laughter if he had known he had been associated with something as macho and as rugged as Scotland Yard!

She passed who she assumed must have been a Police photographer. So, she thought, the Police car wasn't the first on the scene.

"Morning Ma'am. "

"Good morning -what's happened here then?"

"Frederick Sutton Ma'am", he replied, not questioning her authority;probably assuming if she had made it this far then she must have authorization.

"Murdered yesterday evening sometime apparently", he continued, "stabbed in the back with his own letter opener-emerald encrusted if you please", he added with a slight smirk.

"Oh my goodness how ghastly. " She paused..... . "but, I guess if you're going to be stabbed, it may as well be with something that's emerald encrusted!" She immediately regretted the statement, remembering that not a lot of people shared her sense of humour when it came to death-especially murder. After a few moments of unbearable silence..."I'm more of a rubies man myself Ma'am", was his response accompanied by a genuinely friendly smile.

They both laughed-Beth being relieved at his understanding of her humour.

"Tom MacDonald", he said extending his hand.

"Hello Tom, Beth Wade-Beechly", Beth replied with a smile and a firm handshake.

"So what's your business Beth?"

"I'm a Private Investigator based in San Paledino-having a bit of a holiday" (Beth had her story ready) "But, we're a curious lot us 'private eyes', and well, seeing all the action here, thought I might pop in and see if I could help."

"Oh Gawd," was Tom's reply, "don't think Brown'll be very happy-not too keen on women doing any kind of work , out of the house that is-especially if it's work that's going to get in his way."
"Brown?"asked Beth.

"Yes, Detective Sergeant Richard Brown-thinks he runs the show down at Milton Street Station, but as far as I've ever seen, seems to make more noise than do any real work-likes the sound of his own voice if you know what I mean."

If she didn't, she was about to find out.

The door that divided the store and Sutton's office flung open so hard that the door knob left a dent in the wall as it hit. "I'm off then", Tom said with a smile, "got some pictures to develop-nice meeting you Beth , and good luck!" he added, glancing in Brown's direction. "Thankyou Tom-bye bye. "

Beth smiled as she watched Tom return to the street. She thought he must have been about sixty and reminded her a little of grandfather Beech at that age. But any pleasant thoughts were about to be interrupted.

"Right-understood Davis?and I mean straight away-now GET GOING!!"

"Yes Sir!" answered the other young constable Beth had seen earlier. "P. C. Davis Miss", he muttered softly to Beth as he hurried past, "and look out-he's in a frightful mood!"-and in what seemed like a gust of wind, he was gone as well.

Beth took a deep breath and turned around slowly, coming eye to eye with Sergeant Richard Brown.

"Who the hell do you think you are?-and what the hell do you think you're doing here?This is official Police business. "

Charming, Beth thought. "Alright I'll be honest with you. I'm a Private Investigator who tricked the young Constable at the door into letting me in", she replied, never letting her eyes drop. She was also an inch or so taller than the Sergeant which gave her an enormous psychological boost. "If it's going to get him into trouble", she continued, "I'll leave now." "W-well what do you want?" he replied, looking her up and down.

She was 'in'-her frankness had thrown him and she knew it -he was obviously expecting a lie. Still, she didn't let her guard down for a moment. This wasn't a very nice person she was dealing with and she had felt it from the start. "Well as I was telling Mr. MacDonald, I'm holidaying from the United states and curiosity got the better of me I guess and.....

"Yes alright alright cut the crap, can't do any harm I suppose" he snorted "cut and dried case anyway-already picked up the culprit, no need for any Private Investigators-thanks all the same", he added sarcastically. "Come and have a look at the corpse if you like", he said opening the door to the office, with a sickly smirk "*if* you think you can stomach it ", he added under his breath.

They entered the room-a plush office, richly and pretentiously decorated. "More like a museum than an office" Beth whispered to herself.

The body was still at the desk, slumped face down. The letter opener was in full view-the green stones almost glistening in the weak rays of sun which were beginning to stream through the half opened blinds. Beth *could* stomach it -she had certainly seen a lot worse in her time-in San Paledino alone. Hence, she looked straight at the body without flinching and out the corner of her eye could see that Brown resented her for it. "You have a suspect, you say?"

"More than a suspect-not that it's any of your business-she's guilty as sin, this one. "

"She?" Beth turned around to face him.

"*Yes, she* ", Brown replied sarcastically, "some pathetic little *piece* he was servicing-seems he found something better, tried to give her the flick, and she wasn't having it ", he continued, hoping to shock her with his use of language.

Oh please, Beth thought to herself rolling her eyes almost embarrassed for him at his futile attempts. She turned back around to face the body because at this point in time, the sight of a murdered corpse was far more appealing than that of a chauvinistic and obnoxious Sergeant of Police!

"Well", she said. leaving the office and heading for the front doors, "there'll be no objections to my coming down to the station." "Look sweetheart", he half shouted, "I don't really care what you do-just don't even come close to getting in my way. "

Beth didn't feel the comment dignified a response, nor did she turn to look at him. This obviously had the desired effect from the sound of the office door slamming in anger. She gave a little laugh of satisfaction as she walked out and onto the street.

Well well she thought to herself, now I know why I'm here. She assumed that whoever this suspect was, she has no doubt been wrongly accused of the crime-so the task at hand?...to find the real murderer and to prove the woman's innocence. Well I guess I don't have any time to lose, she thought, but, first things first! I can't be expected to do all of this on foot and thanks to my precious big sister I *do* have a valid driver's licence. "

A smile came to her face as she brought to mind all of her favourite things back at Hazelton Road. But there was one thing missing and if she couldn't have it in the year 2000, (she'd been searching for quite a while) then she was determined to have it now. On a mission, she marched straight into the nearest car salesyard she came to and within the hour, was sitting behind the wheel of *the* most sensational 1965 red karmann ghia . Beth's dream motor had just become a reality!After adjusting the seats and mirrors, she was soon happily on her way and after a comfortable night at her hotel, she was ready to face the next day. First on the agenda was Milton Street Station. On her arrival she was quite surprised;the station was actually bigger and far busier than she had imagined. She knew Milton Street as a large station in her own time but had somehow not imagined it to be so bustling some thirty five years before. But, as she was to find, this was only the beginning of the surprises in store for her over the days to come.

On entering the building she was pleasantly surprised to see the familiar faces of the two young P. C.'s she had met at the murder scene.

"Oh good morning Ma'am", said P. C. Somersby in reply to Beth's greeting. "Scotland Yard", he whispered to his co-worker, glancing quickly at Beth over his shoulder. She *did* have the feeling that she might be confronted by the 'charming' Sergeant Brown, something she was certainly in no mood for. Instead, she found herself being greeted by what appeared to be Brown's exact opposite. "May I help you miss?" "Beth Wade-Beechly, good morning", she replied reaching for her I. D.

"Oh yes-that won't be necessary Miss Wade-Beechly....you must be

that...'confounded Private Investigator 'Sergeant Brown was refering to last night", he said with a genuine smile. "Oh I see my reputation precedes me Mr, ...?"

"D. I. Brody-David Brody-and may I make clear from the beginning, I definitely don't share our Sergeant Brown's views on Private Investigators-I've a very good friend in the business who has helped me out more than once I don't mind saying. In fact, I'd be more than happy if you could speak with Miss Morris-even if Brown disapproves-and believe me, he will. She's very upset and perhaps if another

woman, one not in uniform were to visit with her...."
"Yes of course, Inspector, I understand. "

Beth had succeeded sooner and in a much easier way than she could have hoped in contacting the prisoner. "much appreciated-this way then, I'll introduce you. "

D. I. Brody looked to have been around forty five years old, with light brown hair that was very thick with yet no signs of greying. His clothes were inexpensive yet neat and perfectly fitted. He wore a dark brown suit and crisp white shirt with an extremely attractive (Beth *was* big on accessories!) tie pin, holding together a mauve and red paisley patterned tie. (she was also big on paisley!)She couldn't help bringing to mind the shabby overcoat and crooked, sauce-stained blue and gold striped tie of Detective Sergeant Brown.

"In here, Miss Wade-Beechly", he said in a voice that obviously came from many years in the 'force'. It was one that could easily comfort the frightened or hurt but just as easily scare the living daylights out of the guilty if need be. He was good at his job and it showed. "Thankyou", Beth said as he opened the door. He nodded to a Police Constable standing on guard at the doorside. "Constable Forbes." "'Morning Sir", he replied.

"Miss Wade-Beechly is going to have some time with the prisoner", he added. Then, turning back to Beth, introduced her to P. C. Darren Forbes. "If you need anything...." he said before leaving them.

"Yes, thankyou Inspector. . J'll be in touch-and it's a Miss Morris is it?"

"Yes-Susan Morris", he replied.

Beth walked into the room, immediately seeing the fear and confusion on the face of her soon to be client. Sitting on a wooden chair behind a small table was the supposed murderess. Susan Morris was extremely attractive in a fashion magazine kind of way. Her thick bobbed hair was blonde;her eyes piercing blue . She was whippet-thin and in fact, Beth had thought, typified all that was fashionable in 1965. But she wasn't parading on a cat-walk now-nor was she sipping cocktails in an exclusive London night club. At this moment in time, she was a frightened twenty year old girl, whose eyes were puffed from crying.

"Hello Susan", Beth said in a tone that couldn't possibly be mistaken for anything but caring.

After a few moments, Susan's trembling hands reached for the cup of water on the table in front of her. She took a sip and looked up at Beth. She tried to get a cigarette from the packet but her shaking hands just wouldn't permit it.

"Susan, listen to me " Beth took the packet from her, gave her a cigarette and whilst lighting it continued " I'm not a Police Officer, I'm a Private Detective-and I'm on your side. "

"A Private Detective?"

"Yes", Beth went on , "and I want to help you-if you'll let me. "

"I-I think I need your help" Susan said, her voice frail. "But I don't know if I can afford "

"Now don't you worry about that. " She paused for a moment thoughtfully. 'I'll tell you what-I'll make a deal with you", she said with a smile, "you let me help you and find the real killer and once this is all over...promise me you'll give these up?" Susan looked at the cigarette packet in Beth's hand and smiled-a smile that lit up the whole of her face. She knew she had found a friend. "It's a deal. Miss...?..."

"Beth Wade-Beechly at your service" said Beth, giving a playful bow.

Susan drew on her cigarette and exhaled, looking up at Beth as she did.

"I didn't do it Beth" she said, her eyes filling once again with tears.

"I know love, ...and together, we're going to prove it. "

CHAPTER FOUR.

The next day was spent busily searching for as much information Beth could possibly find on the late Mr. Frederick Sutton. By all accounts he believed in living up to every penny he made. He frequently held lavish parties, both in his penthouse and on his yacht and judging by the store names at the top of his accounts, had extremely expensive taste in clothing and self indulgence. Gathering the facts of Sutton's life had filled most of the day, not that Beth had really minded. lt was a good excuse to see some more of London-1965, and an even better excuse to show off her wonderful new car! However at 7 o'clock that night she couldn't deny that she was just plain exhausted, yawning as she entered the foyer of her hotel. On collecting her key she was surprised to find that there was a message awaiting her. "A Mr. Scott left this for you Ma'am" said the night clerk. "Oh thankyou", Beth said as she repeated the name in her head.

She walked up the stairs to her room holding the note. let herself in and sat down to read it. lt all became clearer once she saw the letterhead: BEVAN SCOTT-CHARTERED ACCOUNTANT. She had learned the previous day that Susan had worked as a secretary for Mr. Scott in Thackery Lane-a row of lawyers, accountants and other business firms in the city. The note read as follows: Dear Miss Wade-Beechly,

My wife and myself are both deeply distressed at the situation concerning Miss Susan Morris. We believe, like you in her innocence and would like to help in any way we can. Please contact us so that we may arrange a meeting as soon as possible.

Your's faithfully Bevan Scott.

Beth sat for a moment in thought. Could she use the help or would it be wiser to continue the investigation alone? After weighing up the pro's and con's she finally decided to phone the Scott's household first thing in the morning.

At 9 a. m, she decided it was time and dialed the number provided on the note. Mrs. Scott answered and was eager to arrange a time when they could meet. "Well I'm free all day really" Beth said keenly. "Good, then I'll have Bevan leave the office early and shall we say 2p. m Miss Wade-Beechly?"

"2 sounds perfect but please call me Beth. "

"Beth it is then, and I'm Theresa. "

"Goodbye then Theresa-I'll see you this afternoon. "

She hung up the phone and straight away rang room service to order some breakfast. While waiting for it to arrive, she switched on the radio and couldn't help having a dance around to the tune that was playing. She wasn't quite sure what it was but thought it sounded a little like one of Aunt Dorothy's Hammond Organ favourites! She was however rescued from the entire composition by a knock on the door and was soon sitting down to toast and honey. She poured some tea and sat in the warmth of the sun that was filtering softly through the window. She didn't always eat breakfast, usually just a tea or coffee on the run was all she had time for. But this morning she felt like she needed it-something told her it was going to be a very busy day. She also had a newspaper sent up. She was reading it and becoming furious at the way the story had portrayed Susan Morris. It had made her sound like some air-headed 'dolly girl' who had murdered her lover in a fit of passion. This made her all the more determined to get the case wrapped up quickly so that Susan may try to put it all behind her. She was a beautiful girl and too young to be going through all of this.

She put the newspaper down in disgust, taking a last sip of tea. This morning she would see Susan and get the whole story from her, not wanting to push things yesterday as she was obviously far too upset. She arrived at the station to see D. I. Brody and D. S. Brown exiting one of the interviewing rooms. She stepped back and loitered around the corner to try and hear what they were saying. By the conversation that was taking place, Beth could rightly assume they were refering to her client.

"Give the girl a break Brown-can't you see she's upset?" "Give the girl a break?" retorted Brown. "She stabbed a man Inspector Brody, her prints are all over the murder weapon-she murdered some poor chap in cold blood and I'll be damned if I'll lighten up on her!" "Oh, some poor chap Brown-don't give me that rubbish-you know as well as I do what kind of a man Frederick Sutton was. Look...", he said, regaining his composure, " all I'm saying is that she's just a child and no matter what she may have done-and I mean *may*-she *is* still only a suspect afterall-she's paying for it in fear right now. "

Brown paused then shook his head. "What's your problem, Brody?", he asked in a sickeningly sarcastic voice, "You gone soft or something? or maybe you've just got a bit of a liking for the younger girls?"

"Brown, you disgust me", was Brody's direct reply, "there's obviously no use trying to speak to you rationally. "

It was at this point that Beth decided to make herself seen. She could afterall, only drink so many cups of water from the cooler!

"Good morning gentlemen. " she said brightly as though she had heard nothing of what had been said.

"Oh here we go ", Brown snorted as he left them, "well at least *this* one's closer to your age, Brody. "

The Inspector shook his head apologetically and Beth simply rolled her eyes-no words were necessary when it came to Sergeant Brown. "You're here to see Miss Morris then?"

"Yes Inspector ", she paused, " look may I call you David? and you call me beth?-all this formality business never seems quite real to me. "

"Of course Beth. I wish you would-to be honest I feel quite the same way but I guess it's just something you get used to in this job. "

He lowered his voice slightly and continued...

"Brown's power games have left their mark as usual. Miss Morris is very shaken-I'm sure she'll be glad to see you. "

"Thankyou David. " She entered the room.

"Oh Beth no one believes me, they all think I killed Freddy-I didn't- I, I couldn't. "

She broke down in tears. Beth sat in the chair opposite her, took her hands in her own and spoke frankly. "Susan I know you didn't do it and you know you didn't do it but there's a very determined Police Sergeant out there who is more than eager to lock you up as quickly as possible and wash his hands at this whole case. Now I, for one refuse to give him that satisfaction. "

Susan stopped crying and sniffled. "But what can we do?" she asked, her voice husky and dry. "You have to pull yourself together-and I mean right now. Blow your nose, have a cigarette-if you must- and I'll get us a cup of coffee. By the time I get back I want to see you dry-eyed and ready to tell me all about you and Mr. Sutton, alright?" She stopped and turned at the doorway. "I know it's painful Susan- but you have to be strong. "

Susan nodded and reached for a handkerchief.

Beth stood for a moment in the hallway, trying to get her bearings.

"Need any help Ma'am?" asked a friendly but efficient voice behind her.

"Oh, Constable Somersby", she said with a smile, "actually I was trying to find a cup of coffee!" "Well I can certainly help you there Ma'am-follow me. "

Beth walked beside him as he made pleasant conversation all the way.

Lee Somersby was about twenty five years of age but really didn't look a day over eighteen. He was tall and well built with neat blonde hair and a very honest face. She momentarily wondered if Sergeant Brown had ever started out as a fresh-faced honest young 'bobby' like this but quickly dismissed the thought. He was from a different mould altogether, she decided.

They reached the cafeteria and Beth said her thankyous.

"My pleasure Ma'am " he leant slightly lower and in a softer voice added, " anything for Scotland Yard. "

"Oh-er yes, Lee thankyou. "

Beth remembered her little white lie as he walked away. She wanted to call him back to explain who she really was but at the present moment it was more important that she return to Susan.

She soon returned with the coffees and two egg sandwiches.

"Here-when's the last time you ate anything?" she asked, handing her the bag. "You can't get by on nicotine and caffeine you know. "

She suddenly felt a slight twang of guilt as she realized she'd been doing practically the same thing for the past couple of days. It must have showed, as Susan took one of the sandwiches and handed the other back to Beth.

"Okay" Beth began, getting as comfortable as was possible in the chairs provided. "Now, I know you were in the office and I know that your fingerprints were found on the letter opener but I need you to tell me how this came about."

"Alright."

Susan took a deep breath, let it out slowly and began.

"Freddy and I have been...."she looked down at the table...*had* been seeing each other for about five months. It really was just like a fairytale-candlelit dinners, romantic walks in the park-he was very good to me Beth", she said lifting her eyes towards her, "no one knew him like I did, he wasn't a bad man really they didn't know him. Nobody understood him like I did-he was always telling me that", she said, smiling at the memory.

Beth nodded sympathetically and felt sad for the girl. She'd done enough digging for herself to know what sort of a man Frederick Sutton had been. She wondered how many other innocent young girls he had mislead, used for his own ego and then dumped whenever he grew tired of them. How many others were the only one who 'truly understood him like no one else....'? She realized she was becoming angry and so wiped the thought from her head. Anger would only get in the way. Besides, she thought helplessly, the world is full of Frederick Suttons-but at least this one can't destroy any one else's life.

"I couldn't understand it ", Susan continued, "he called and asked me to come to his office-that there was something important we needed to talk about. " She hesitated then continued, "I feel stupid now but I . . I. . thought he was going to ask me to marry him." "Go on ", Beth said listening intently.

"Well naturally I hurried straight over. I walked into the store (he had left it unlocked for me) and straight through to the office. He was waiting for me, and was opening the day's mail. "

"With the emerald letter opener, " Beth stated more than asked.

"Yes" said Susan, tears coming to her eyes. But she pulled herself together and went on, "Freddy smiled at me but it wasn't his usual smile and I knew something wasn't right because he didn't leave his desk to come and kiss me. I thought he may have been ill so I went around to him but when I went to kiss him he pulled away. "Darling, what's wrong?" I asked. He told me to go back around and sit down as he had something to tell me. I still had no idea he was going to break it off-oh I feel so idiotic. such a fool."

"Susan, you are no fool. . men like Frederick Sutton are very clever-you were only following your heart", Beth said encouragingly. "Well then he told me-just like that-he said he'd found someone else. someone that really mattered. " The sadness turned to anger in her eyes. "He laughed at me Beth-when I started to cry, he laughed at me and told me to grow up,"

Beth felt sick for her and for the person he must have been.

"Susan, why were your fingerprints on the letter opener?"Beth asked. "When he'd finished with the letters he placed the opener down in front of him, between the two of us. When he told me to grow up I was so angry that I grabbed the thing and stabbed it into the table. Freddy didn't even blink-just sat there saying how childish I was being." "Did you tell the Police about all of this?"

"Yes I told Sergeant Brown but he just laughed and said " so you stabbed the table first?-nothing like a practice run. "

"Typical" Beth said "well go on Susan. "

"Well that was it. I was too upset to say or to hear anymore so I left-and he was alive when I left Beth-I swear it. I didn't touch him. Somebody must have come in later and..." .. but her tears wouldn't permit her to finish the sentence.

"Well", said Beth taking Susan's hands once again, "I going to find that person-don't you worry,.. everything will be okay. "

Susan stared at the wall. "I really thought he loved me. "

Beth looked down at the table-she didn't know what to say.

CHAPTER FIVE.

It was 1.50p.m when Beth arrived at the Scott's home. Mrs. Scott answered the door and immediately Beth liked her. "Beth?" "Yes, Theresa?"

"That's right, come in-Bevan's not long arrived home himself-he's upstairs changing. "

Beth followed Theresa in. "What a lovely home", she said taking in the surroundings.

"Thankyou. . I really am more of a home-body than anything else. I always think it's the only place in which one can totally relax." "Oh quite so, I thoroughly agree", said Beth bringing to mind the coziness of Hazelton Road. Her thoughts were broken by a baby's cry. Theresa smiled, "And now that Katrina is with us, everything seems complete-even *if* a lot noisier!", she added standing to go toward the crying.

"I've got her!" came a loud and happy voice from the top of the stairs.

"Well, while I'm up I'll make us some tea. You two can introduce yourselves-excuse me won't you Beth?"

"We will indeed my dear", replied a very jolly looking figure whom Beth could only assume was Theresa's husband. "Bevan- Scott Beth, very pleased to meet you", he said shaking her hand so hard that she almost began to rattle. "Hello Bevan and this gorgeous little creature must be Katrina." "Certainly is-isn't she grand?"Very proud of this little one, we are- aren't we?yes we are . . yes we are ", he said drifting into a mouthful of baby mumbo-jumbo.

Beth laughed;she didn't need to be told just how proud, it was written all over his face. Bevan Scott was a big man-not overly tall, but rather rotund(and probably always had been). He had a full head of sandy-orange hair with a beard and moustache to match. He seemed a happy man, with the kind of face that looked like it was either going to blush or burst into laughter at any moment. Beth felt very comfortable in their home.

"Terrible business all this, Susan's a lovely girl. Been with us two years now oh. fellas like that Frederick Sutton make my blood boil", he said looking lovingly at his little daughter.

Beth knew exactly what he was thinking-no one like that was ever going to get near her-not if he had anything to do with it.

"Had you met him Bevan?" Beth asked.

"Oh yes a few times. enough to know that I didn't like him....here", he reached for a photograph from a side cupboard, "this was taken at the office Christmas party just three months ago....look at him" he added "all full of himself-gold chains and no brains-that's what I always said. "

"Bevan!" Theresa said half sternly . carrying a tray of treats from the kitchen.

"Ah there she is-love of my life", he said successfully avoiding any further scolding.

Theresa shook her head at Beth. "Talks before he thinks does our Bevan. "

Beth smiled-and at several decibels louder than necessary!-she thought to herself. But, if that was to be his only crime then good luck to him. By the looks of the other photographs around the room Beth assumed that they must have been together for quite some time. They were both at the least in their late thirties so it was no wonder that this little orange-haired bundle had brought so much joy into their lives.

"Katrina was my old mum's name-we named the little one after her", Bevan stated out of the blue.

"Oh that's nice" Beth replied sincerely.

"Oh honestly Bevan-he's obsessed with her you know", Theresa laughed.

"Oh and I suppose you're not old girl!" he replied jokingly.

Theresa offered Beth a biscuit and placing the plate back on the table, began

"Beth Susan has been well she really *has* been like a daughter to us hasn't she love?" Bevan nodded, biting into a chocolate wafer. "Neither of us liked this chap Sutton from the start", she continued, "but young Susan was smitten. She was from the country-came to London two years ago looking for work *and* I'm afraid, not knowing much about life if you know what I mean. Luckily, Bevan was looking for a secretary at the time and well, like I said she's been like daughter to us ever since. "

"That she has", said Bevan, "we love her like one of our own Beth, so anything at all we can do-just ask." "Well for a start, you could let me borrow this picture for a while. "

"Well of course, if it will help in fact, we've a couple of copies left over haven't we love?"said Theresa.

"Say no more my darling I'm on my way. "

"Bedside table I think love-and Bevan, turn that set off on your way will you?", she added a little louder as to be heard. She turned to Beth. "I've never known what all the fuss is about when it comes to that television-give me a good book anytime!. Bevan loves it! ", she laughed rolling her eyes, "but if you ask me there never seems to be anything worth watching. "

Beth simply laughed. Oh how she wanted to tell her new friend to 'hang in there'. . that 1967 will see the arrival of Emma Peel in 'The Avengers'! A life-size cardboard figure of a leatherclad Diana Rigg had recently found a new home Beth and Sarah's apartment. She smiled to herself remembering Sarah's reaction to it's arrival!

Time passed quickly and Beth found herself enjoying the Scott's company more and more by the minute. They had proved to be genuine, open-minded people and Beth began to feel like she'd known them for far longer than just one afternoon. "I must go", said Beth eventually. although not at all looking forward to the cold wind awaiting her outside.

Theresa stood up, flinching slightly as she did. Beth noticed earlier that she was limping a little but hadn't felt the need to comment.

"Alright love?" Bevan asked. "Yes I'm fine- really." "Had a bit of a fall in the bath did the old girl", Bevan explained to Beth, "slipped over right on her. . "

"Yes alright Bevan-I think Beth gets the idea!"

Theresa laughed but somehow not as naturally as the laughter Beth had heard all afternoon. Had something just happened that Beth wasn't aware of?A word-a look-an action that she had failed to pick up on?Whatever it was the mood in the room had definitely changed-only for an instant but it *did* change. Beth was sure she hadn't imagined it.

"I'm just glad I didn't have the little one in my arms", Theresa added, hurriedly tidying up the tray on the coffee table.

Beth didn't let her curiosity show as it was clear that Theresa was feeling uncomfortable although Bevan hadn't seemed to notice.

"Well, thankyou for a lovely afternoon", Beth said standing, "....and thankyou for this as well", she added looking closely at the photograph.

She walked to the door with the whole family and said her goodbyes.

"I'm so glad Susan has you two" she said "and I promise I'll be doing everything I can to prove her innocence-and as quickly as possible. "

Beth kept up her smile until the door closed between them. She jumped into her flash new vehicle and sat-puzzled. "What on earth just happened in there? "Something wasn't right. She felt tired. . confused...she needed the comfort of familiar surroundings.

She temporarily put the Scott's out of her mind and drove to her hotel. She flopped onto the divan, cushion under her head and feet up on one of the armrests. She took a long deep breath and slowly closed her eyes. Within moments she was in exactly the same position on her own comfy sofa at Hazelton Road.

"Jesus Beth!!!", was Sarah's sudden scream, "can't you and Grandma devise some kind of warning system instead of just popping up?-I was just about to sit there!

"And hello to you too, Sarah" was Beth's cheeky reply. "What did you have in mind?-some kind of a beeper?...or maybe we could install a radar system - now *that's* a novel idea..."

"Yes alright", Sarah cut her off , "but you could at least reappear in your own room-what if I had guests?" "Mmm, true enough", said Beth, "point taken. "

Sarah looked at her slightly suspiciously as if not quite believing that her sarcasm had ended there.

"Oh-yes-well", she continued when she realized that it had, "welcome home Beth how's it all going?"

"Strange, Sarah-just a few things I have to work out. "

"Well..... don't wear yourself out doing it, you've got plenty of...'time!

excuse the pun!" laughed Sarah.

"Hmmm yes-very amusing, Sar's. "

"All nonsense aside though Beth", Sarah continued. still chuckling at her own joke, "you look a little tired;don't wear yourself out-why don't you go and see Beverly-that always cheers you up. "

A smile came to Beth's face. "What a great idea, that's exactly what I need. Sis, I'll be a couple of hours then I'll ring Gran and maybe we can have dinner here later?"

"Lovely, see you later then. Oh and Beth ", Sarah smiled, "....Mr. Edwards rang again this morning. "

"Oh great, what this time?"

"Ready for this one?He wants you disguise yourself as a dog-catcher and kidnap Maxine so that he can prove Mrs. Edwards incapable of responsibility and gain total custody!"

Beth was momentarily lost for words. All she could do was raise her eyebrows, open-mouthed. "And I thought *I* had troubles in the 60's!-see you sis.

"Hello stranger!" came a friendly voice from the kitchen of Cafe Good.

"Oh hi Bev" Beth smiled, "I suppose it *has* been a few days." "Oh only a couple-you look tired, Love." "I am Bev-strange sort of case", Beth answered thoughtfully, "but....you know the rules-can't go into it. "

"Say no more how about a nice cup of camomile 'on the house'. "

Beth sat comfortably and happily in the 'safe' surroundings of the cafe , but her mind was on Theresa Scott. She may have been back in her own time but her thoughts were still firmly planted in 1965.

Suddenly Beverly burst through the swinging doors. "Beth, Beth!....something terrible's happened ....in the kitchen!!"

"What-what?!!". shouted Beth immediately jumping to her feet.

Bev put her arms on Beth's shoulders and looked into her eyes.

"I dont know how to tell you this but. . we've-we've run out of chocolate mud cake", she said breaking into a smile and bowing to the on-looking kitchen staff's applause.

"Oh you so and so!" Beth said and flopped down laughing, "you know I always think the worst in my business!"

"I know", Bev chuckled, "I'm sorry sweetie but I thought it might cheer you up-bring back that gorgeous smile!"

And it did just that-and took Beth's mind temporarily off the case. Sarah was right!-a visit to the Cafe Good was exactly what the doctor ordered!

So after polishing off a gigantic piece of banana cream pie (Bev's attempts to get back into the 'good books') Beth rang Selina. Selina was naturally delighted to hear from her grand daughter and eager to hear all about the case.

Over a wonderful vegetable curry and bottle of white wine at Sarah's and Beth's apartment, Beth filled her sister and Grand mother in on all of the details.

"Sounded like rather an unsavoury fellow, dear" said Selina, listening intently.

"Mm", agreed Sarah reaching for the rice bowl. I'll bet he had *lots* of enemies. "

" Oh yes I'm sure of it but only one of them killed him", Beth said anxiously.

"You'll get to the bottom of it", Selina said proudly, "you always do. "

"Emerald encrusted", Sarah murmured quietly to herself. Then snapping herself out of it asked, "so *was* he seeing somebody else, Beth-is that why he broke it off with Susan?"

"No, I don't think so Sar's. I think that was just an excuse ;but I'm sure there would have been soon enough. "

"Yes", joined in Selina, "men like that don't stay lonely for very long. "

"Mm even so", considered Beth, "It's worth looking into yes yes, you're right Sarah-no stone unturned and all of that!"

"That's the spirit girls!" said Selina.

"And also, I'm going to pay a visit to Lillian Sutton-Frederick Sutton's ex- wife. to see if *she* can throw any light on the subject. "

"You're not going just now though?-you need to rest", insisted Sarah.

"No. no I've done enough running around today-I'm going to spend the night right here in my own comfy bed. "

Beth turned to Sarah.

"Thanks for your concern though, Sis. "

"Concern nothing, Beth", she smiled, " it's your turn for the dishes!"

CHAPTER SIX.

Beth, in fact stayed another day and night in San Paledino but after reading Maria's postcard from Rome and finishing off her second decaf, she decided it was time to return to the past. She must talk to Susan again and do some more delving into Frederick Sutton's private life. And so, by lunchtime, she was back in carmen(she had now named the car) and was once again cruising the streets of London in 1965.

Beth was in a good mood;she had touched base in Hazelton Road and was feeling happy. Today might just be the day that something breaks, she thought. She adored her new car and was singing quietly as she drove. Ever since she had learnt she was returning to the sixties, she hadn't been able to get Petula Clark's 'downtown' out of her head (although at this point was wishing she could-it was beginning to drive her mad!) She could have happily let her thoughts run wild and just drive around the whole day long. However she had a case to solve and she wasn't about to solve it from behind the wheel of an 1965 Karmann ghia-no matter *how* gorgeous it was!

She returned to her hotel, lay on her bed and propping herself up onto one elbow, proceeded to write a list of things to do. On top of the list was to speak with Sutton's ex-wife Lillian.

Lillian Sutton wasn't hard to find. She was what a lot of people would refer to as a 'social butterfly'. Constantly in the gossip pages of *all* the newspapers and known throughout London for her lavish charity benefits held monthly at her inner-city apartment. But it wasn't to the penthouse that Beth was heading today, but rather to the beautiful little village of OakWillow-to Lillian's country home-a two hour drive north east of London. The journey not only gave Beth time to clear her mind for the day ahead, but also gave Carmen a chance to have areally good workout....obviously a little *too* good!

She was having a wonderful time until about three miles out of the village where upon she was stopped by two members of the local constabulary.

"Uh-oh" she said to herself, "what to do-talk about my work and hope to goodness they don't have a chip on their shoulders about Private

Investigators-or just keep my mouth shut?Well, here they come deep breath. "

Beth got out of the car and was quite relieved to see two very young male P. C's. Piece of cake!, she thought. She *had* imagined another D. S. Brown and was sufficiently hyped for the situation. But this looked like it was going to be easy! "Hello there Miss", said one of the Constables, 'l think we might have been going slightly over the limit. "

"Yes Officer, if you say so then I quite believe it", was Beth's reply, "to be honest I've not had the car long and well, really I'm still getting used to her."

"She's a beauty Miss", replied the other P. C. . momentarily forgetting he was actually at work, "...must be a dream to drive. "

"Constable Nolan is a little obsessed with cars-you'll have to forgive him, Miss Wade-Beechly", said the first Officer reading Beth's driver's licence.

"I know how he feels-I'm a bit that way myself'. Beth laughed. "Anyway", she continued, "as I said I'm sure I did exceed the speed limit but I have an appointment at Sutton Lodge and I'm afraid I became slightly lost-I guess I just didn't want to be late. "

"Sutton Lodge?", was the quick reply. "Well that's only about ten minutes from here-you're a friend of Mrs. Sutton?"

"Er no, I'm I'm a Private Investigator and I need to speak to her about the death of her ex-husband. "

"Oh yes we've all heard about that. Does a lot for this community, does Mrs. Sutton-gives a lot of money to the school-and paid for a new hospital just last year. I don't know what we would have done without her really. "

He paused for a moment then smiled. "Look, if you promise to keep your eye on that new speedometre of yours, we'll forget about this little matter alright?" "Sounds good to me Constable....?...." "Jones, Miss." "Well thankyou vey much Constable Jones. "

P. C. Jones was clearly a 'hometown' boy, probably born and bred in OakWillow or nearby and as proud as punch of the fact. Beth thought that this may be a good time to throw in a few complimentary remarks about the local surroundings-never hurt to get on the right side of the 'powers that be'-especially in a town this size! She proceeded to do so and whilst praising the cleanliness of the area, noticed out of the corner of her eye that P. C. Nolan was crouched down looking under the car. "Beautiful machine", he said to himself.

Constable Jones smiled and rolled his eyes. "Look I'll tell you what-things are a bit quite today so to make sure you don't get lost again. why don't we drive out to Sutton Lodge and you can follow us...nice and *slowly* !", he added smiling.

"Oh that sounds wonderful....but...", Beth continued with a grin, ". . I've got a better idea-why don't you drive me and Constable Nolan can follow us in the Karmann Ghia. "

P. C. Nolan suddenly looked liked a five year old in a toy store and immediately jumped to his feet. "Well I think he's happy about that Miss!"said Constable Jones laughing.

Well old girl, thought Beth as she stepped into the Police car-another potential fine mess you've gotten yourself out of!

On arriving at Sutton Lodge she said her goodbyes and thankyou's.

"Thank *you* ! " said a beaming Constable Nolan as they drove off happily to uphold law and order in 'bustling' OakWillow.

Beth turned to the house after waving them off. "Wow. . will you look at this" she said aloud "it's fantastic!"

The house at the end of the path was like something, she thought from a story book-Hansel And Gretel meet Scarlet O'Hara immediately sprang to mind! This mansion was surrounded by individual grass hedges shaped into everything from Big Ben to the magic pumpkin from Cinderella. "I don't believe this ", she said in a whisper and with a grin.

On the way to the front door she passed a Rolls Royce which was the most unusual dark pink in colour. Parked next to it was a silver Jaguar and Beth had to wonder just how many more there were. She couldn't wait to get inside the house to check out the interior. She pressed the doorbell and was treated to the first few lines of 'the girl from Ipanema' in xylophone form. Beth got the giggles and by the time the door was answered after the third rendition, she was near to hysterics!

"Hello!-I really love your doorchimes! I'm Beth Wade-Beechly." "Hello love, so sorry to keep you waiting. I was on the phone, bit of organizing to do- never a dull moment around here." "Not to worry", Beth said shaking her hand and following her in. "Lillian, is it?"

"Yes love drink?"

"Oh just a soda water for me thanks. "

"Lovely.. I'll pop a slice of lemon in that for you-you won't mind if I have something a little stronger though?"

She's wonderful, Beth thought to herself-just wonderful. Lillian was a bottle-blonde, and as brown as a berry (a tan kept permanent, Beth was later to discover, by regular visits to her villa in Spain) . Her face was fully made up with the brightest of green eye shadow and lips as red as they come. She was wearing an obviously fake leopard skin low cut top, black tights and white backless stilettos, all topped off with an obviously not so fake string of pearls.

On the wall of the living room was a hugh tapestry depicting a bowl of lillies that included the phrase. . 'to the most beautiful lilly of them all'. Unlike Sarah , Beth she was never much of a tapestry fan . In fact the only reason she ever allowed the 'Taj Mahal' to remain on the wall of the sunroom at Hazelton Road was because of its pure kitsch value. (but not that Sarah was aware of this)!

"Sit down love", Lillian said cheerfully sipping on a pink concoction of ice, fruit and what smelt like half a bottle of gin.

She handed Beth her glass of soda and made herself comfortable on the sofa opposite.

"First of all Lillian, "Beth began, "might I say how very, very sorry I am for you at the loss of your ex-husband. "

"Huh!", laughed Lillian . . 'first of all-call me Lil-all my friends do. . and second-Don't be!, Oh I'm sorry pet", she continued, "I know you mean well and I appreciate it but to be honest with you the world's a better place without that bastard. "

All Beth could do in reply was to smile. She wanted so much to agree but thought that a little *too* unprofessional at this point in time.

"That no good cheating stealing rotter!-I always said someone would do him in one of these days.

He's damned lucky it wasn't me, the pain he's put me and my boy through over the years." "Boy?-you have a son?"

"Yes love" she said, her face lighting up, "Our little Glendon-nothing like his father-a real good boy our lad. Sure he's been in a bit of trouble over the years, nothing serious mind-and I tell you what, he looks after 'is mum-always said he'd give his old man a clobberin' one day-one that'd pay him back for all the one's he's given us. " Beth winced.

"He hit you?"

"Yes love-hit me, cheated on me, stole from me...for years it went on", she said frowning at the memory. "Then one day I looked in the mirror and said Lil my girl, you're worth so much more than this. So I packed his bags, marched straight into that fancy office of his and told him not to bother coming home because he didn't have a home to come home *to* no more!"

"Good for you!", was Beth's prompt reply. "So it was you that left him? Well I'm pleased to see that you managed to do quite nicely out of the divorce settlement", she added looking around the room.

Lil looked puzzled then laughed. "oh Pet, you've got it all wrong-*HE* was the one that did okay. That brute came with nothing and left with his own home and a jewellery store. " She paused and smiled softly at Beth. "You don't know who I am, do you love?-what I mean is you don't know my maiden name?"

"Er...no I don't", said Beth slowly and quizically.

"It's Dulfer. "

"Dulfer?!", Beth repeated, almost choking on her water.

"Yes chook-*now* would you like something stronger?" she laughed.

Beth laughed in return.

The name was as instantly familiar to her as it would have been to any one in her field.

"Are you telling me that your father was "

Lil finished the question for her. "Sammy Dulfer? Yes the one and only-God rest his dear old soul."

She smiled to herself then looked back at Beth. "Now, I know he did a lot of wrong in his time but he treated me and me old mum like royalty-his Queen and little Princess-that's what he used to call us. "

A tear came to her eye. "Besides, he paid for his crimes with those last five years-killed him you know-died of a heart attack 'inside'. But I suppose you'd know about all that."

"Yes . . I'm sorry. "

The words just slipped out automatically from Beth's mouth (and she immediately hoped they sounded sincere.) Sammy Dulfer had been one of the biggest and most feared crime bosses of the thirties and forties, with a hold over most of Northern England and Scotland, as well as rumoured dealings with notorious crime families in europe. M. I 5 had eventually nabbed him with some kind of loophole in the law-something to do with tax evasion, Beth remembered. He was sentenced to seven years but served only five before his death in 1954. He and his associates were responsible for far worse crimes but nothing could ever be proved-not with the amount of judges and senior Police Officers he had on his payroll. So basically the aim became to just get him off the streets, which they eventually succeeded in doing. So this is all gangster money, Beth thought to herself, looking around the room again. She quickly snapped herself out of her surprise and returned her thoughts to the moment. "As I said, that bastard came with nothing and took, took, took."

"So can I ask what brought you together in the first place?" "two bottles of champagne and a moonlit picnic, that's what! A real smooth talker was our Freddy-knew all the best lines and when to use 'em. Huh!-bit stuck for words though when I told him he was going to be a daddy!!" "Oh I see", said Beth.

Lil took another sip of her cocktail and continued

"Ran away he did, like a scared little boy-left town for two whole weeks!"

"And then he came back?"

"Came back alright-with a huge diamond ring. a sweet smile and a very well rehearsed marriage proposal-Daddy's fella's had paid him a visit you see. Oh don't get me wrong, he was quite happy to marry me once he saw the perks. You see Daddy was an old fashioned fellow-of the firm belief that if a man got a woman 'into trouble' then it was his duty to marry her and even though he never liked Freddy, he demanded that he do the right thing by his 'little Princess'. "

"Right I see-so Sutton was looked after by your Father?"

"Oh yes", Lil replied, picking out a strawberry half, "set him up in the shop-had him trained and all-he would have been nothing if not for us", she added bitterly, " nothing!"

"Well", said Beth, "there must be money in the jewellery trade-he seemed to be living quite the high life. "

"Pet, "Lil replied sighing, "Frederick Sutton never did an honest day's work in his life. I'm sure there *is* money to be made in jewellery but you can bet your bottom dollar that *his* money was dirty. Who knows what else he had 'is filthy hands into. "

"Well "said Beth thoughtfully, ".......perhaps his death could be gangland related?"

"I-I don't understand", said Lil, "I thought someone had been arrested. "

"Well yes someone has", explained Beth, "but I'm not convinced it's the right person. "

Lil stood and took a last mouthful. "Well I'm for another-how about you love?" "No thankyou Lil, I must be off-It was really lovely meeting you", she added. (Not that she would have said anything else to a crime boss's daughter!) But she really did mean it. Lil Sutton was one of the most genuine people she'd met in a while. "Come and see me again won't you pet?-and next time off duty so you can join me in a *real* drink!"

"I'd like that"said Beth.

They reached the door and whilst saying their goodbyes, Lil asked, "Tell me-this lass they've arrested, is she alright-how's she coping?"

"She's holding up, but just-she's quite young and very confused." "Young? How young?"

"Twenty."

"Oh my lord-and with a son only two years older!"

She shook her head in disgust and added, "Well you tell her from me love, if she has done it, she's done a hell of a lot of people a *big* favour. "

Beth gave a slight laugh. "Bye then Lil", she said.

Stopping after a few paces. she turned and asked "Lil, does Glendon live in London?"

"Oh no love, up North-got his own shop he does-sells motorbikes-nothing he doesn't know about the things!"

"Ooh how wonderful-do you see him much?"

"Not since Christmas pet I do miss him. "

"Yes I can imagine. Well bye then-and thanks for the drink!"

Beth just loved this part of the country-the colours, the tiny villages, the curling and winding roads. She had often thought she'd like to have a little cottage up this way sometime in the future. "Well", she chuckled, "the *future* future!"(she really *was* quite easily amused.)

"Oh I don't need to go back to London tonight", she said to herself, and before she knew it, was pulling into a guesthouse and checking in for the night.

Glendon Sutton was on her mind. She had quickly dismissed the idea of a gangland killing as it just didn't have the signs she'd seen so often of that kind of thing. But Glendon Sutton-now this was something to definitely think about. " Always said he'd 'pay him back one day'", she said aloud, remembering Lil's words.

After a sleep, wash and change of clothes (she was always prepared!) Beth decided to do her thinking whilst taking a stroll down the village's main street. She was still thinking of Glendon Sutton and had also remembered that Lil had said she hadn't seen him since Christmas. Not that that necessarily meant anything, she thought. Just because you happen to be in town murdering your father doesn't mean you have to pop in on your mother as well!

Pretty soon she found herself at the door of what looked to be a very cosy public house. There was a fire burning and only about twenty or so patrons inside. Popping her head a little further inside the door, she immediately recognised one of them as the car-loving P. C. Nolan, sitting with a young woman who looked to be about the same age as himself.

"Oh hello there!", he called, spotting her at about the same time, "come and join us. "

"Hello again now I only know you as P. C. Nolan, but I'd guess you'd have a first name as well?!"

"Yes", he laughed, "It's Anthony-and this is my girlfriend, Nancy Briers-W. P. C. Briers actually . The place is crawling with us!"

"Hi Nancy, I'm Beth", she said shaking her hand and sitting down.

"Hello Beth-you're not from around here are you?"

"No darling, this is the lady with the Karmann Ghia!"

"Oh I see, so you're to blame", she said smiling, "he hasn't stopped talking about it all evening-ever since he picked me up from the station!"

Beth laughed. "You're stationed at OakWillow as well?"

"No, I'm at Chipwick-on-Hemming, about fifteen miles from here-lovely village. If you've time during your stay, I'd love to show you around-never a lot happening at work-very quiet little place." "Oh I'd love that", Beth said in reply, "thankyou!" "Now, what are you drinking Beth?", asked Anthony. "Ooh half a bitter for me please-, but I'm paying for this round-it's the least I can do after my little 'let off 'earlier today!"

"No let him pay Beth, he's loaded-everyone knows how corrupt the OakWillow Police are! Same again for me darling." "Ha-Ha-Ha", he said jokingly, "nothing like a bit of healthy station rivalry, eh Beth?!"

Beth and Nancy chatted and on his return from the bar, Anthony reminded Nancy of the topic they had been discussing earlier in the evening.

"Oh yes, "she began, "your murder victim-I knew him. Well, met him once anyway-that was enough. "

She shuddered and pulled a face. "Nancy's originally from London-that's where she met him", Anthony added.

"Go on, "said Beth intrigued.

"Well, it was about five years back now, we hadn't long left school-one of my friends, Jillian was seeing him for a while. It was a surprise to most of us as he was almost twice her age...but i think she just saw him as man of the world. He really messed her up Beth and I mean badly. He got her into alcohol, drugs-you name it. Oh he promised her the world but it didn't last long-he soon got sick of her and called it off . Well unfortunately he not only left her with a broken heart but also a severe drug dependency. Her family had to pay for her to go into a rehabilitation centre. " She paused and shook her head. "Later we found out that she had been pregnant but had lost the baby-I guess she was just too run down, both mentally *and* physically. It almost destroyed her. . Ive never seen such sadness-she was broken. I remember at the time. her father just went totally crazy-burst into Sutton's office one day and knocked his lights out and I don't blame him! Everyone was so surprised because he was such a calm man usually." "Well good on him I'd say", Beth said listening intently. "Yes I agree", added Anthony.

"Oh yes indeed", continued Nancy, "but anyway, Sutton was actually going to have him charged with assault! It was only on advice from his lawyers that he didn't-probably would have been bad for business I suppose. "

"Mm, that's so sad and now?", asked Beth, "Do you still hear from her?" "Oh yes-she's a strong woman Beth;she's been hurt deeply and of course his death will bring it all up again for her, but her family is wonderful-they've really looked out for her...she'll be okay." "Ooh", said Beth angrily, "the more I hear about this Frederick Sutton, the more I dislike him. It sounds like he made a habit out of treating young women like this. "

"Yes you're right, "answered Nancy, "it's just a shame there weren't a few more Tom MacDonalds around." "Tom MacDonald?" "Yes-Jillian's father. "

Beth paused and thought for a moment. "I met a Tom MacDonald in London-at the scene of the crime in fact. "

"That's him-a Police photographer isn't he love?", Anthony said turning to Nancy.

She drew her eyebrows together.

"That's odd-we spoke about the murder, only briefly granted, but he didn't mention anything about knowing the victim." "I expect he just wants to forget", said Nancy, "probably thought justice had now been done and wanted to leave it at that. "

"Yes. . yes of course", replied Beth, not totally satisfied.

After that, the conversation lightened and they all enjoyed a very pleasant evening. Beth couldn't keep herself away from the jukebox-it was absolutely packed with all of her favourites-although at 'last drinks', she felt that if she had played Cilla's 'You're My World' once more, she may have been physically evicted and so, resisted the temptation! Besides, the Elvis lookalike by the snooker table had started 'making eyes'-Now was the time to leave.

That night back in her room, she took out a notebook and titled a page SUSPECTS. Her thoughts went on Did you finally pay your father back Glendon-once and for all? And you Mr MacDonald. . yes justice *had* been served-but by whom? She again put pen to paper and under the heading wrote GLENDON. She put the note book down and gazed out of the window at the night sky. A few moments passed before she picked it up again.

"I hope so much to be wrong", she said aloud, and reluctantly added the letters T-O-M.

CHAPTER SEVEN.

The next morning was sunny and fresh and the countryside looked wonderful. Beth wondered what kind of a day it would be in San Paledino. It was quite early and as it was such a lovely day, she decided to take up Nancy's offer to be shown around nearby Chipwick-on-Hemming.

As she had rightly predicted the night before, things *were* very quiet and so the two women enjoyed a lovely hour's outing around the town and surrounding countryside-followed by tea and biscuits back at the station. After after yet another round of thankyou's and goodbye's Beth was once again back on the road and heading for London. lt was time to get 'cityfied' again and as much as she hated doing it, she must find out what she could about Tom MacDonald and his feelings toward the late Frederick Sutton. First stop on the agenda was Milton Street Station. She parked Carmen, approached the front door and was harshly reminded of the reasons why people move to the country-to escape a certain kind of people for one!

"Get out of my way!", was the greeting she received from a very irate looking Richard Brown. On his exit he kicked a waste paper basket flying and violently knocked a vase of plastic flowers from the inquiry desk. He turned on his heels at the door and yelled, "Get off this case you hear?-none of your damn business!"-and with an almighty SLAM! he was gone.

"And a good morning to you too Sergeant", replied the ever-so-calm Beth, much to the amusement of the surrounding officers.

She headed for the cafeteria, picked up two cups of coffee and a bag of jam doughnuts and made her way up to D. I. Brody's office. Before she had time to knock, he opened the door. "Beth!-hello."

"Oh you're just leaving?"

"No, no-well only to get a cuppa and unless I'm being over presumptuous, something tells me that one of those could be for me?" "Yes here we are, and I hope you like doughnuts-oh of course you do-all Police officers like doughnuts!"

"Well as it happens", he laughed, 'I do!...come in...but am I also sensing a case of impending attempted bribary??

"Well yes I'm caught out!", Beth answered smiling, "I *was* hoping to have just a few minutes chat with you. It's nothing about Susan Morris-well not directly-so you won't be put on the spot professionally. "

"Sounds interesting, what would you like to talk about?"

"Well it's actually about one of your Police photographers. "

David smiled. 'Tom MacDonald", he stated more than asked. "I don't know how you Pi's get your information but you always seem to dig it up as quickly as we do!" Beth was tempted to say ' MORE quickly usually' but held her tongue.

"Let's see, "he began "correct me if I'm wrong you *somehow* discovered that Tom's daughter Jillian was abused by Sutton and you're afraid that finally

Tom MacDonald may have taken revenge on his daughter's behalf." "Perfect so far", Beth said nodding her head slowly. " and you, along with the rest of us, like Tom so much that you were scared of discussing what you've discovered." "Exactly!, " Beth confirmed, 'and that's why I came to you. You see the only other person in authority I've met around here is Brown and after the greeting I just received I wouldn't go within ten feet of him !"

David paused then smiled. "Well, I appreciate that Beth but I can happily tell you to relax. As it happens, Tom himself came to see me on the morning after the murder, as he was worried for the same reason. He knew we had a suspect but wanted to clear his name just in case. We talked it all out and I told him to forget it. He's a good man Beth. I've known Tom for quite some time and believe me-he's no murderer. As you've no doubt heard. he *did* assault Sutton-but I'm sure you also know why." "Oh yes, sounds like something quite a lot of people would have liked to have done." "Mm, I think you're probably right-under the circumstances. Well...happier now?" he asked reaching for a doughnut.

"Yes", smiled Beth, a lot happier thankyou. "You know if I wasn't trying to prove Susan's innocence, I wouldn't have bothered bringing this up at all. It doesn't really sound like the world's any worse off for Frederick Sutton's passing-but I'm so glad you were able to tell me what you have. "

"Well I'm glad to be able to put your mind at ease!"

They chatted for a few more minutes and when the conversation turned to D. S. Brown's attitude. It was explained to Beth that he had been carrying more than a slight chip on his shoulder after losing the Inspectors' position to D. I. Brody just six months earlier. "We actually trained together you know. "

He paused then shook his head. "Sometimes I wonder just where the years have gone." "Yes I know just what you mean", was Beth's reply, considering momentarily her up and coming thirty-fifth birthday!

As she took a bite of her doughnut, the phone on the desk rang.

"Yes?-yes fine-on my way-and see if 'uniform' can spare a couple of faces we may need all the help we can get. "

He placed the phone down and looked at Beth apologetically.

"I'm sorry I'm going to have to leave you-duty calls. Stay though and finish your coffee", he added puting on his jacket. "Thanks David and thanks for the chat." "That's quite alright-thanks for the doughnuts! Bye now. "

He stopped at the door. "Oh and Beth, *do* try to stay out of Sergeant Brown's way for the rest of the day-not a very happy man by all accounts-a bungled stake out. One that he had *demanded* to be put in charge of and it's all gone terribly wrong. So, as you can imagine, he's in more than just a spot of trouble with the powers that be. But having said that, I'm sure *you* can handle our Mr. Brown! See you later. "

Beth took a sip of coffee and smiled. She hadn't found the killer but she still had another suspect left. She relaxed in her chair and felt happy-Tom was off the hook-the sky was blue-*and* there were still two doughnuts left!

CHAPTER EIGHT.

On the way home to her hotel that evening, Beth found herself driving toward 'Sutton's Fine Jewellery'. It was cold now. The blue sky had vanished and London felt gloomy . It was one of those days when everybody seemed to have their heads down just hurriedly getting on with their business and back to the warmth of their homes.

She stopped at the opposite side of the street and looked across at the store. How quickly, she thought, can everything change. One day Frederick Sutton was 'Mr. Big'. riding high in the lush life he had manipulated for himself-the next-dead-murdered in his very own office. "I really must be a bit nicer to Sarah", she laughed, "or at least remember to hide her letter opener!"

She was immersed in her own thoughts and ideas when a voice suddenly surprised her.

"Nice car Miss", said a small boy bouncing a ball and staring wide-eyed at Carmen.

"Oh thankyou-she *is* nice isn't she?"Beth replied smiling. "My name's Beth, what's your's?" "Tommy, Miss-Tommy Talbot. "

Tommy looked to be about ten years old but quite small for his age. He was well prepared for the weather, with a bright red scarf and matching mittens. Beth couldn't help but smile at the large dried mud patch on his little grey trousers-it had obviously been quite a day in the playground! "Do you live around here Tommy?"

"No Miss I'm just waiting for my Dad-he works for the bank just up the road here. "

"Oh I see. . so you play around here a bit then?"
"Yes lots-just while I'm waiting for Daddy to finish work. "

Tommy happily bounced his ball and hummed a few bars of a song , he explained to Beth , that he had learnt at school that day. Beth smiled and thought 'what a cutie!'. Suddenly he stopped and pointed across the street. "You see that shop? A man got killed there." "Yes", said Beth smiling at his innocence, "I've heard about that. "

Well I was here that afternoon-and that very night he got 'done in'! I've seen him too-he was *really* rich. "

"Yes", said Beth nodding, remembering parts of her conversation with the lovely Lil.

"I know lots of people in this street", Tommy said proudly. "I've even seen his wife-she's really pretty she is...she said hello to me once. "

"Yes, she's very nice", replied Beth smiling at his assumption that all couples were naturally married.

"Do you know her Miss?"

"Yes I do, Tommy and I agree-she *is* very pretty."

Tommy pulled a bag of sweets from his pocket and offered one to Beth.

"She was sad the other day-crying she was. I thought that maybe they had a fight or something. "

Beth suddenly became more interested in the conversation.

"When was this Tommy?", she asked. "Day he got killed Miss." "And you saw her leave the store crying?"

"Yes Miss it made me sad. "

"I'm sure it did Tommy. Can you remember if she was by herself?-think hard now. "

"Yes-well yes-except for their little baby. "

"Little baby?", Beth repeated sounding confused.

"Little baby Miss-you know- chubby little thing-bright orange hair! ", he said smiling. "I even know her name", he added with even more pride in his knowledge, "it's Katrina. "

A car horn honked from a not too far away distance.

"There's my Dad-I have to go Miss?"

"Oh-oh yes. Bye then Tommy. ", said a half dazed Beth.

Tommy had confused his married partners but he hadn't confused what he had seen. It wasn't Susan Morris he had been talking about but somebody else known to Beth. "Theresa", she said aloud. What on earth was she doing at Frederick Sutton's office after hours *and* more than once?An affair was surely out of the question-she and Bevan seemed so happy together and yet one never really knows. Her thoughts continued...."you knew him through Susan-but *why* were you crying??"

She realised there was only one way to find out- a visit to the Scott's household.

By this time it was too late as Bevan would have been home from work and Beth wanted to talk to Theresa alone. She decided to sleep on it and face it all again in the morning.

Early the next day, Beth drove straight to Bevan's office in Thackery Lane just to make sure he was there.

"Good morning! ", said Beth on entering the office.

"Well well, hello there Beth!", was Bevan's cheerful reply. "What a lovely surprise. I was just catching up on some Thackery Lane gossip with Marjorie here-you've well and truly caught us at it! Marjorie Burgess-Beth Wade-Beechly. "

The two women greeted each other and Marjorie explained that she was a friend of the family's and was filling in until Susan was back at work.

"Which won't be long with super-sleuth Beth on the case!", added Bevan with a smile and a wink.

God, Beth thought to herself....is this man *always* so cheerful? "Well. I'm doing my best", she replied, "have you seen Susan?"

"Yes. Still very upset-very scared...and apparently there's a particularly nasty Policeman hanging about the place. "

"Yes I know exactly who you mean. "

Beth, now knowing that Bevan was definitely at work, was more than anxious to talk with Theresa and so quickly made her exit.

"Well Bevan I only really popped in to say hello and to tell you that I've been off following up quite a few leads. "

"Oh good-well call in again Beth anytime. Now I suppose we'd better get on back to work ourselves-can't stand around gossiping *all* day!"

"Goodbye Marjorie-and don't let him work you too hard!"

Bevan roared laughing. 'Good lord' Beth thought. . and people say *I'm* easily amused!

He saw her to the door and as she was descending the stairs, she turned and casually asked...."so you and Theresa didn't really know Sutton all that well did you?"

"No, as I said I'd met him a few times when he'd come to pick up Susan and well, Theresa had only met him at the Christmas party last year." "Okay thanks Bevan-bye for now. "

She sat in Carmen and thought long and hard. How *ever* was Theresa Scott connected with Frederick Sutton? This obviously had something to do with the sudden mood swing at their home that day. Beth had quite a few questions-and hopefully some of the answers would be just a drive away.

She pulled up outside the house and wondered how to approach the situation. Her thoughts however were soon disrupted by Theresa's voice and a gurgle from the pram. "Hello Beth", she said happily, "we've just been off for a walk, haven't we Katrina?" "Hello Theresa. "

Beth wasn't about to pretend that nothing was wrong. She respected this lady far too much to try to trap her with any tricky detective talk. "Theresa I need to talk to you-can we go inside?"

"Well yes, come in but Bevan is still at work. "

"Yes I know-it's actually you I came to see", replied Beth, holding the door open for her.

"Oh", replied Theresa in a slightly worried tone, "well, just let me get the little one down and we'll have some coffee. "

"Fine-but I'll make it-then can we have a chat?"

Beth didn't want to waste any time making small talk or waiting for coffee to be made. She intended to get straight to the point-although at this moment was feeling a little sick in the stomach. What if Theresa *had* murdered Frederick Sutton?She liked this woman-and in proving one 'decent' human being's innocence, was she about to prove another's guilt?

Theresa returned after a few minutes and Beth had the coffee ready. Little Tommy was right-Theresa *was* "really pretty"-in fact she was quite beautiful-but at the present moment she looked scared-her hands trembling as she reached for one of the cups.

"Theresa", Beth began taking a deep breath, "why were you at Sutton's Fine Jewellery on the day of the murder?"

Theresa's eyes filled with tears-she wasn't about to hide a thing.

"Oh Beth", she said, "how did you know?"
"Someone saw you leaving-just a person on the street." "I. . I see", she nodded blowing her nose.

"Theresa, please tell me what's going on-I don't want to have to start working for you as well as Susan!", Beth said smiling to try to lighten the situation.

"Oh, you mean oh God, I never thought of that you mean *I* could be a suspect?"asked Theresa frantically. "I only wanted to keep Bevan from knowing-that's why I couldn't say anything."
"Whoah, hold on Theresa-you've lost me. Now, deep breath, dry your eyes-I'm not here to upset you, I just need to hear the story-the *whole* story. "

"Alright."

Theresa took a sip of coffee and began. "Beth I have a wonderful life. I'm very fortunate. I have Bevan, Katrina and I don't know if you know this, but we've a small fashion business on the side-and I do mean small-you know just word of mouth basically. I make the clothes that Susan designs. We've become quite popular around the city;oh nothing too exciting but we've managed to sell quite a few designs-all one offs-I think that's the attraction really. Well, my point is that things were going rather well for all of us."
"Were?"asked Beth , pensively.

Theresa continued

"About six months ago, Bevan came home devastated. You see six months prior to that he had been encouraged to invest a substantial amount of money into a certain company. It seemed to be a sure thing and Beth, Bevan is a sensible man-he would never have risked what we had if he hadn't have known what he was doing. Well things went terribly wrong-due to one of the top men basically absconding with the company's fortune. Oh the Police tracked him down quick smart but that didn't mean we saw any of our money again. We weren't the only ones to lose out either, many of Bevan's associates were also affected-some of them far worse than us. So as I said, Bevan was totally devastated-still is-though he'd never show it on the outside. He's such a proud man and it hit him hard. He felt that he'd 'done wrong' by Katrina and me-that he'd let us down. "

"Yes I can imagine but what has this to do with Frederick Sutton?"

"Things were getting worse. Bevan was becoming more and more depressed and the banks refused to give us any more money. I was desperate, I didn't know where to turn. Neither of our families ever had more money than they needed for themselves so we couldn't ask them for help-not that Bevan probably would have anyway." "Oh right-think I'm beginning to get the picture", said Beth nodding to herself.

"I was desperate Beth and then at the office Christmas party, the idea came to me. I spoke to Susan about possibly asking Frederick for a loan. Well, she said she thought that he would be happy to help-and he was-more than happy . The amount of money we needed was nothing to him and I realised he was out to 'win me over' in regards to his keeping company with Susan-as he knew we looked upon her as a daughter. Well, naturally Bevan couldn't be told any of this as he would have flatly refused to go along with it. So, a few days later, Susan and I went to see Frederick to organize the terms of the loan-which were very good-although like I said, he would hardly have missed the money. I was to pay back an amount each month which I've only done twice-once in February and then in March. "

Beth looked puzzled into her coffee cup. "Well all that seems straight forward but Theresa why were you crying when you left the office on the day of the murder?"

Theresa looked down at the floor. "Oh Beth", she continued looking back up, "I feel so degraded- so, oh I don't know just so disgusted at the whole business."

"Why? What happened?", Beth said slowly-the anger growing inside her, "what-did-he-do?"

"When I arrived with the second payment he was different-cocky-you know, real sure of himself . He'd obviously been drinking and heavily ...it was horrible.

She paused. "Go on", Beth encouraged.

"Well that's when he started making suggestions-saying I could pay him back in other ways-that sort of thing. I was so shocked and angry that I just threw the money on his desk and turned to walk away . Then before I knew it he had left his desk and was blocking my exit...he grabbed my arm and pulled me into him . I told him to let go as he was hurting me but that only seemed to encourage him. I was so scared Beth -the store was closed and I knew nobody else was around. He was becoming angry and shouting at me and the more I struggled the tighter he held me. Sudden he just laughed and shoved me away, but so hard that I fell onto the floor- and all of this in front of the baby-I think that's what upset me the most." "So that explains the limp", Beth said shaking her head in disgust.

"Yes and I couldn't tell Bevan-I don't even want to think about what he may have done. "

"Theresa, how did you explain acquiring the money to Bevan in the first place?"

"I told him that one of our customer's lent it to us-a boutique owner-of course I made up a name as I knew Bevan would never check. He wasn't at all happy at first-mainly that an outsider knew of our financial situation. But then after a while I could see how much more relaxed he was becoming, just knowing that we were out of 'deep waters'.

"Oh Theresa that must have been so hard for you having to lie...but now tell me, what time did you leave the office? Please think carefully-this is very important", Beth stressed.

"It was almost six o'clock-about ten minutes to I would say. I know that because I intended to be home before Bevan and he usually arrives home about half six. "

"Well then you can relax-Susan was there after you -which means we won't have to go to the Police and of course this also means we won't have to tell Bevan any of this. "

"Oh thankyou Beth. I can't tell you how it feels to have this off my chest. I've been sick ever since it happened-mainly because I've never kept anything from Bevan in my life-I just feel so guilty. "

"Hey none of that! You were only doing what you thought was best for your family", Beth quickly reassured her. "Um Theresa", she asked slowly, "only you, Susan and I know about this loan right?"

"Yes that's all. "

"Well I'm not going to tell anybody and I'm sure Susan won't. And let's face it-

Sutton's *definitely* not about to spill the beans! ", she said with a grin, "I think this means you're out of debt!"

She paused to think of a cover plan. "Just keep on taking the monthly payments so that Bevan won't be suspicious and buy something for the home or for little Katrina-he wouldn't notice that would he?"

"No", laughed Theresa, "not our Bevan!"she added smiling for the first time in a while. "Thankyou Beth you're a true friend. It's such a relief to have all of this out in the open. "

"Well I'm glad Theresa and you know that if ever you need a chat-about *anything*-you can reach me at my hotel room." "Yes that's great Beth. "

"There's just one thing", added Beth, "have you told Susan about Sutton's behaviour?"

"No because that very day he was murdered and she's been so upset ever since I haven't had the heart-but don't you worry-I will one day. "

Beth was so relieved at the fact that Theresa wasn't the murderess that she gave into the temptation she had been resisting since the first day she had arrived in London-clothes shopping!!There were just so many wonderful little shops that she just couldn't hold back any longer. A good coffee-and clothes-Beth's two big weaknesses!. After two solid hours - and a strawberry milkshake stop-, her mind was now cleared enough to head for Milton Street Station for another chat with Susan. She returned to the hotel and after giving herself a mini fashion parade, once

again headed out, happily sporting her brand new dark green corduroy jacket.

On arrival at the station she gave a wave to P. C. Somersby who was at the other end of the carpark. He was just getting into a Police car with P. C. Davis, who also turned to wave. "Still here?", Sergeant Brown snorted as he passed Beth in the hallway.

I wonder if that man has any friends, she thought to herself, ignoring him.

"Hello Susan", Beth said on entering the interview room. "How are you holding up?"

"Oh Beth I'm alright I suppose but all of this sitting around just gives me time to think about Freddy."

Beth wanted so much to tell Susan of 'Freddy's' behaviour toward Theresa but resisted-the last thing she needed right now was for Susan to turn against her. Besides, she thought, Theresa would choose the best time to let her know.

"Susan I need you to promise me something-from now on you must tell me everything you can think of-and I do mean *everything*-that is in any way connected to Frederick Sutton. "

"What do you mean?", replied Susan looking slightly puzzled;slightly worried.

"What I mean is I've spoken with Theresa and I know all about the loan the two of you arranged with him." "Oh I see-does Bevan know?", she replied.

"No and I'm not going to tell him but you must tell me these things. I *am* on your side you know and although you may not think that certain things are important, they may well be. If I'm to find the real killer and get you out of here then I don't have time to run around town finding out these things for myself. "

"I'm so sorry Beth I just didn't think at the time- it didn't seem to be of any importance to the case. "

Susan suddenly looked uncomfortable-her eyes dropping from Beth's to the floor.

"Susan?" Beth paused then rolled her eyes. "Okay-what is it you're not telling me?" "Oh Beth don't be mad. "

"Susan what is it?"

"Well", she began slowly, "on the day I saw Freddy I was so angry that when I stabbed the desk...well I also took something from it. "

"You what?!"

"oh I knew you'd be mad. "

"It's alright. . it's alright, darling I'm not mad", Beth lied and quickly composed herself, "just tell me what you took. "

"Well", continued Susan, "all I could think about was that there was someone else and when I had first arrived Freddy had been looking in something and before he saw me had put it down on the desk. it was a small green notebook and as I stabbed the desk in anger it occurred to me that 'her' name must be in there. "

"Go on", said Beth shaking her head.

"Well while he was still laughing at me and telling me to grow up he looked away for a moment-just long enough for me to snatch it before he noticed. "

"Susan", Beth said, "I can't believe you didn't tell me this-why on earth didn't you tell me this?"

"I thought ", she hesitated, " I thought you'd think I was young and stupid that I was just a jealous kid-that's what *he* called me. "

She started to cry.

"Heeey", soothed Beth, "I'm not mad at you and I don't think you're stupid-far from it-lots of people would have done the same-possibly even me!

Here..... have one of your nasty old cigarettes", she added amazing herself at actually encouraging the habit. But after all, Beth had been a smoker once herself and so could easily relate. "Thankyou Beth you've been so kind-I don't know where I'd be without you and the Scotts. "

Beth smiled and lit her a match. "Susan where's the notebook now?"

"It's at my apartment. I was so embarrassed by what I had done that I hid it-in the lining of one of the bedroom curtains." "Hmm I must remember that trick", said an intrigued Beth raising one eyebrow.

"Well I didn't want anyone I knew to see it and to think I was being silly." "Right, so that's obviously why the Police haven't discovered it . So did you read it? *Was* there another woman?I bet there wasn't." "No-you're right-there wasn't. Just a few names and addresses-mainly of men, and a couple of businesses." "Well I'd like to take a look at it . "

"Of course Beth but how will you get into the apartment? The Police have the keys." "You let *me* worry about that Susan", she said with a cheeky smile. Her thoughts continued, sister Sarah may be 'tops' in the forgery department but no one gets inside a locked door like Beth Wade-Beechly!

"Okay Susan I'll do that tonight-now keep those spirits up. Can I get you anything-a newspaper-ooh no I guess not, sorry. How about some magazines or books?"

"No Beth really I'm fine-thankyou though. "

"Well how about....", Beth reached slowly into her jacket pocket, " this!!?Guaranteed to cure the blues", she added pulling out a huge block of chocolate fudge. "Just don't let Brown see it-he'll think I've slipped a file inside!"

Susan laughed and gave her a hug. Beth was pleased she'd made her happy-even if only momentarily-she genuinely cared for Susan and always liked to leave her with a smile on her face. At the door she turned and smiled "anything else to tell me young lady??"

"No Beth-I *promise* !"

CHAPTER NINE.

Beth (as predicted) successfully (and rather easily) gained entry into Susan's apartment and retrieved the small green notebook from exactly the place Susan had described. Naturally she worked in the dark and had only her torch for light. When leaving the bedroom when she was startled by a noise. A figure that appeared to be entering the front door momentarily froze in its tracks then suddenly dashed off. Beth was startled and so a few moments passed before she sprang toward the door. But whoever it was had vanished down the hallway and back out onto the street. "Who the hell was that?", she said.

The figure was dressed in black and Beth couldn't make out the form of the body-so wasn't even sure if it had been a man or a woman. She went back to the bed, sat down and thought for a while. 'I think you need a break old girl. . and there's no place like home.

She drove back to her hotel thinking she had better not mention the incident to Gran- it would worry her terribly.

"Now", she laughed to herself, "do NOT reappear on the living room sofa!", remembering the scolding she had received the last time. This time she did as Sarah had requested and appeared in her own bedroom. She quickly looked out to see if there any guests and on seeing that the coast was clear began

"Beep...beep...reappearance warning to Sarah Wade-Beechly beep beep...."

After a slight initial shock Sarah looked around and smiled.

"Oh now that's much better Beth-how are you darling?", she added kissing her on the cheek, Im so pleased to see you. "

"Well I'm fine", Beth said suspiciously, "but why are you in a such a cheery mood? Don't I at least get into trouble for being a little 'smarty pants'?"

"Not today, no", she replied smirking.

"Okay sister mine-what's going on??"

Sarah, hard as she may try, never really *could* hide anything-especially from Beth! "Well....just come into the office today that's all. "

Beth was stumped-she wasn't used to Sarah being in control of a situation and her face suddenly took on the appearance of a spoilt five year old.

"No I won't!", she said, "Not until you tell me what's going on", she added, pouting.

"Oh Beth you're such a spoil sport. Alright-Mr. Edwards has insisted on coming into the office today....", she looked at her watch, "...in half an hour's time in fact. He wants to discuss new 'strategies'..... and well, now that you're here....", she said smugly, "Come on!"

Beth had to think quickly. She looked to the ground.

"Well well-stuck for words are we?", Sarah laughed, "Come on then-there's no getting out of it this time!"

Beth said nothing but started to follow her sister toward the door. Sarah stopped in her tracks.

"Beth-you're actually coming?-without putting up a fight? I don't believe it", Sarah said proudly, realising she had her trapped.

Beth simply smiled, continuing to say nothing. "No", said Sarah, "this really is too good to be true-something's wrong isn't it?"

"I'ts nothing" "No Beth...what is it?" "Well...... . I just had rather a nasty experience back in London;run in with an intruder. Oh I managed to come out of it okay but to be quite honest j'm still a little bit shaky. In fact that's why I came home-to see you and to relax-you know, to try and put it out if my mind. "

Sarah frowned , apologetically. "Oh Beth I'm so sorry. I didn't think you were quite yourself-and me going on and on. Well you do just that then-put your feet up and watch some television-and you know where I am if you need me." "No Sarah I'm being a big baby. I can't keep on letting you do my dirty work. "

"Now Beth don't be silly . You've had a fright-I can see how upset you are-I shouldn't have been teasing you like that. No, you stay here and rest-I can handle our Mr. Edwards!"

Beth paused. "Thanks Sar's-I really appreciate it-you do know that don't you?", she said sincerely.

"Now enough of that. What else are big sisters for?"You have a good rest you hear?And I might even consider cooking dinner for you tonight." "Thanks so much Sarah-love you. "

Beth closed the door behind her and proceeded to let out the laugh she'd been holding in for the last five minutes! "Aah the number of Oscars I could have picked up over the years!", she said heading for the kitchen. "Now a hot chocolate i think is in order!" She couldn't help but feel a little guilty-but only a little!

She made her drink, flopped onto the sofa and decided to phone Selina to plan out the day. After arranging to meet her Grandmother for lunch, she suddenly felt very tired..."this time-travel really takes it out of a girl...days becoming nights...nights becoming days-I dont remember what day it is half of the time". She was mentioning her predicament to Eartha Kitty , the resident siamese , who naturally wasn't all that interested. She did however give Beth a token 'meoow' in reply. . before yawning and returning to her favourite sleeping position.

Beth drifted off but before too long her alarm was reminding her loudly and clearly that it was now lla. m in San Paledino and time to wake up.

She (as always) had a wonderful time with Selina-lunching, shopping-and of course discussing the case. Now , back at Selina's apartment, Beth showed her Grandmother the notebook and like Susan had said, it contained the names, phone numbers and addresses of what they could only assume to be business associates, whom Beth intended to investigate immediately on her return.

"Well my dear", said Selina , "time for me to rest these old bones. I'll have Rex drop you back at home. Not going into the office?" "No-for some reason Sarah insisted I stay away and rest today-isn't she sweet?", Beth replied looking closely at the notebook.

On Sarah's arrival home Beth was so engrossed in a rerun of 'Here's Lucy' that she'd completely forgotten about their conversation that morning.

"Hi little sister!", was Sarah's cheerful greeting, "You look more relaxed now-how was your day?"

"He he! I love this show...come and check out Kim's fabulous outfit! Um yeah my day? Great, we went....oops!", she stopped mid sentence.

"We?!", Sarah asked sternly, "we? went...?...I thought you were going to rest and recover from your ordeal! Beth Wade-Beechly, if you've been lying to me "

"Oh alright I'm sorry Sar's", Beth whined, "I admit it. I wasn't really all that shaken up-but there *was* an intruder!"

"Ooh you little rat!-you never change do you? You made me deal with that fool of a man while you were what?-gallivanting around the city I suppose!"

"Um something like that", Beth replied and falling to her knees continued "Please forgive me Sarah please pretty please??"

"Oh knock it off!", She said with a hint of a smile. (Sarah was *also* quite easily amused.) "Honestly Beth one of these days..... yes alright I forgive you but think yourself lucky! Anyway I'm too hungry to be angry-some of us had to work right through their lunch break." "Great! I'm hungry too-and because you're such an understanding big sister, I insist on buying you dinner." "ooh Lovely-no need to ask where I suppose-I'll get my coat. "

Naturally enough as Sarah had predicted there was no need to ask where dinner would be eaten. They arrived at Cafe Good and headed straight for Beth's favourite table. "Well if it isn't the Wade-Beechly sisters! How are things with you two?", was Bev's ever-cheery welcome as she sat down to take their order.

"Good thankyou Bev-Beth's paying tonight. She's trying to make up for a stunt she pulled on me today. "

"This Beth?", replied Bev jokingly, "she'd never do anything naughty would she?"

"You don't know the half of it Bev. "

"Yes yes alright you two-when you're quite finished ganging up on me-I'll have the usual thankyou. "

" And I'll have the same thanks Bev", added Sarah feeling quite pleased with herself.

"Oh hello girls!", Bev called toward the door.

"HOWDY BEV!!!", came the reply in chorus with more than a few 'yeehaa's' thrown in.

"Oh Lord it's those bloody boot-scooters", said Beth rolling her eyes.

"Hey that's enough out of you-they're paying customers-now behave!", said Bev playfully tapping the top of Beth's head.

"Boot-scooters?", asked Sarah intrigued.

"Yes you know Sarah, country and western dancing. ", Beth explained, "I forgot what night it was-they come here after class", she added once again rolling her eyes and smiling cheekily at Bev.

"Don't pay any attention to her Sarah-she thinks it's silly but it's a great laugh. . I've been trying to get her to come along to a class for ages now. "

"Yes well you'll be trying for a lot longer yet!"

"I think it sounds like fun", said Sarah turning to look in the group's direction.

"Now why doesn't that surprise me?", Beth mumbled.

"So can you do this boot-scooting Bev?", asked Sarah.

"Well I try-I go along to classes whenever I can get the time off from this place. "

"Well give us a demo then, lady", Beth teased- "you know you want to!"

Bev happily obliged with a few quick steps then bowed to the applause of all 30 members of the 'Eastside Rainbow scooters'

"Alright then I'll admit it-very impressive", Beth said, joining in with the clapping. After dinner both women were far too full to move and so relaxed and chatted for an hour over a pot of hot fruit tea, afterwards deciding to walk their meal off and head home. Beth loved the city at this time of the evening. Always so much going on-she so enjoyed the buzz. "Well goodnight then Bev-thankyou for another wonderful meal", Sarah said holding her stomach. "See you soon old girl!", Beth added with a wink.

"Real soon okay?", called Bev smiling, "..... " and not so much of the 'old'"!

CHAPTER TEN.

As much as she would have liked to have stayed longer in San Paledino Beth was anxious to make her way through the notebook to see what she may (or may not) discover. And so after a call to Maria who had arrived home safely from Italy, she was once again transporting herself back to 1965.

She made herself comfortable back at her Hotel room and began to dial the first of the phone numbers in the notebook. The dozen or so numbers she had rung so far had turned out to be quite reputable businesses (or were known to be). She could see a possible connection or how there could be a reason for all of the names and numbers being in Sutton's possession. 'Gina's Travel soon turned out to be 'Gina's escorts', a busy inner city agency. She wondered if Sutton had been an owner or a customer-or possibly both.

There was still one number left. Whereas all of the other's had a name or at least some initials proceeding them, this was on it's own. She reached once again for the phone and dialed, reading the numbers from the page.

"Redlands Crematorium", was the response, "how may we help you?" "Er-sorry wrong number", Beth replied, swiftly placing down the phone with a shudder.

"Ugh!", she said to herself, "How may you help Frederick Sutton is the question. "

A cold shiver ran over her as she started to imagine how a man with Sutton's criminal connections may benefit by having a 'friend' in the crematorium business. She began to feel quite ill and so immediately wiped the thought from her mind.

Later that night she decided to take a drive down town to 'Gina's' to see what she could find out. She picked up some Chinese food and parked herself across the road from the establishment. She liked doing this kind of thing-made her feel like a good and proper detective! She began to jot down a few quick descriptions of punters, nearby cars, licence plates and so forth. While removing the lid on her container of rice, she was suddenly surprised (but at the same time not surprised) to see a very familiar face attempting to leave the premises as discretely as possible.

"Oh this is too good to be true", she said to herself and within seconds was across the road and directly in front of a very startled Sergeant Brown.

"Good evening Sergeant Richard Brown of Milton Street Police Station!', she said extra loudly. "Come here often??"

He came to within inches of her face and Beth soon realised by the smell of his breath that he was more than just a little intoxicated.

"Yes", he said swaying, "as a matter of fact I do you smart-arsed little "

"Lovely!....", Beth cut in, "....and *Mrs.* Brown knows about these little visits does she?"

"Mrs. Brown", he slurred, "does very nicely in the kitchen little Miss Private Detective but the ol' girl's lacking a bit in the room that really matters-if you know what I mean. "

Once again his futile attempts to shock and offend Beth had failed miserably and she simply yawned in his face. As she did she had the strong feeling that if she were a man he would have punched her....she only wished he would have tried.

As he stumbled off muttering under his breath, Beth marched straight up the stairs and into the foyer. She walked to the front desk and picked up one of the agency's business cards. "Could I take one of these?" '"Of course love", nodded one of the women inside, looking Beth up and down. . "we cater for all. "

Beth smiled and returned to her car.

The following morning after talking with Susan, she saw the opportunity she'd been waiting for. Sergeant Brown was stomping down the hallway (in usual form) in the midst of yelling some orders to a very fed up looking W. P. C.

"Oops!!", said Beth banging straight into him and at the same time slipping the card from 'Gina's' into his shirt top pocket. She kept on walking but glanced back to see a stunned and irate Brown and a smiling W. P. C. She mentally patted herself on the back and imagined the nice little surprise Mrs. Brown would be getting next washing day!

The rest of Beth's day was spent checking further into the numbers that she had rang from Sutton's notebook. One number was that of a young local thug by the name of Lenny Hill. She had managed to obtain some information on him from a couple of street kids at a down town snooker hall (but only at the cost of five pounds). Lenny apparently did 'odd jobs'-a bit of car stealing, courier work and the odd spot of breaking and entering-not to mention a number of assaults. Apparently he had been doing 'very nicely indeed' since being put onto Frederick Sutton's pay roll. Word was that he went from driving a beaten up Morris minor to a rather snazzy Jaguar E-Type within a matter of weeks. Beth had concluded that because of his inclusion in Sutton's personal group of names and numbers that he must have been his 'top boy'. She thought to herself well, 'he's out of a job now'. She then paused...'or is he? He obviously had contact with Sutton on a regular basis. What if someone had offered him a better job?(On condition that he was to get Sutton out of the way?) It was a real and valid possibility. . but if so...who? And if that *were* the case then surely *he* would be after the little green book! Right-tomorrow I find out just where our Mr. Hill was at the time I saw the figure at Susan's apartment.

Then....she would tackle the mystery of the crematorium.

Beth parked Carmen at the front of the hotel, headed up the stairs to the entrance and feeling energetic, decided to take the stairs instead of the elevator. With key in hand she reached the fifth floor and walked toward her room. Then- in a sudden flash! she was grabbed from behind, a leather glove placed over her mouth. Startled but not panicked she instantly remembered what Maria had always told her daughters-in a situation like this-go limp and drop. She did just that and slipped from their grasp to the floor. With all the strength she could muster, she threw an adrenilin fuelled punch so hard into their groin that she actually hurt her hand. Whoever it was then doubled in pain for the three or four seconds she needed to get to the safety of her room. Once inside she leant, puffing with her back against the back of the door.

"Balaclava or no balaclava.', she said aloud with a dry smirk, "...at least I *now* know you're a man."

Not a lot of sleep was to be had that night. Beth dreamt of stupid things-nothing that made any sense. She tossed and turned for what seemed like hours-eventually deciding to get up at 5. 00a. m. She listened to the radio and watched from her window as London also slowly began to awaken.

"So", she said yawning, "what on earth's in store for you today old girl?"

She felt stirred up-angry. No one had the right to do that to her-no one.

Later that morning she headed once again for the source of her information on Lenny Hill (pound notes in hand). Her hopes however of pinning the blame for the attack on hill were dashed when she learned that he'd actually been holidaying in Blackpool for the past few days.

"Damn!", she said in anger as she got back into the car. However she soon calmed herself enough to think rationally and to realize that although he wasn't here in person he could easily have paid someone to attack her-and that he still may well have been in town on the day of the murder.

"Oh I don't know", she said letting out a huge sigh, "come on Carmen, we're getting out of this town for a while. A nice country drive is just what *we* need. "

Beth remembered her 'let off 'in OakWillow the last time she decided to go for a country drive and so this time stuck meticulously to the speed limit(as frustrating for her as it was)! 2 hours later and back in the city she drove passed 'Sutton's Fine Jewellery' , turned the car around and parked directly across the road . Getting out to buy a newspaper, she heard a familiar voice. "Oh hello young Tommy! We meet again." "Hello Miss. !"

"Aha", said the man he was with, "you must be the 'nice lady with the car' or was that the 'lady with the nice car'?!"

"Yes", laughed Beth, "probably the latter!-Beth Wade-Beechly. . how do you do?" "Hello I'm Gavin Talbot-Tommy's dad", he said shaking her hand. "Car mad is our Tommy-knows all about them-makes, engines, you name it he knows about it. Going to own a Rolls Royce one day aren't you son?"

"Yes that's for sure...best car ever made. . and i want one just like the one I saw here the other day-pink it was -lovely dark pink. "

"Pink? A pink Rolls Royce, Tommy?", asked a startled Beth, "When was this then?"

"Yes Miss-funny colour eh? Same day I saw the lady with her little baby. You know Miss-day that fella got done in." "Come on then son, I told Mum we'd pick up some dinner." "Oh great-fish and chips!!!", Tommy said excitedly.

Gavin rolled his eyes and smiled. "Nice to have met you Beth." "Yes Gavin, likewise", she added, her thoughts elsewhere. "Bye Tommy. "

"I can't believe this ", she laughed to herself, "I wonder if that kid needs a job! "

She paused then nodded slowly.

"A pink Rolls Royce I can only remember seeing one of those in my life....Carmen, young lady-I think tomorrow we might be in for yet *another* country drive. "

CHAPTER ELEVEN.

Bright and early the following morning Beth made the decision to speak to Lil before thinking anymore about the elusive Mr Hill. She must find out why Lil was there and most importantly, at what time. She felt a little apprehensive-what if the Dulfer heiress *was* the killer? Was she being totally stupid going out there alone? But soon she was within a couple of miles of Sutton Lodge and had no intentions of turning back. She still felt that Lil was 'real'…but either way, was about to find out as she pulled into Sutton Lodge and parked next to the car in question.

"Hello love!". called Lil from the front entrance, "I saw you coming up the drive. "

"Hi again Lil-I'm sorry I didn't ring first. "

"Come on in I've just made some tea. "

The two women sat down but before Beth could think of how she going to approach the matter, Lil continue , "Oh Pet I'm so glad you've come to visit-truth is I was about to try to find *you*. . "

She put her head in her hands then looked back at Beth. "Lil what's the matter?-I can see you're upset."

She slowly poured some tea and taking a deep breath began "I'm afraid I wasn't totally honest with you the last time you were here. "

"Go on", Beth said not knowing what on earth she was about to hear.

"Well remember you asked me if I saw Glendon often-I told you at the time that I hadn't seen him since Christmas?" "Yes", said Beth encouragingly.

"Well I lied-but only because you'd also just said that you didn't think they'd arrested the right person which meant they were still looking for someone and if they found out that Glendon was in town that day they'd be straight onto him. Beth I know what some of these coppers are like-they'll arrest anybody if it means closing a case quickly. "

"So Glendon was in town on the day of the murder?"

"Yes love but my son's no killer...Like I told you before, he's been in some trouble with The old Bill but what young lad hasn't? He's got himself straightened out now-got his own shop and a lovely little girlfriend-and he's no murderer. ", she added once more almost as if to try to convince herself.

"Why are you telling me this now Lil?"

"Alright love, here's the whole story "

Beth took a sip of tea and waited for Lil to begin.

"On the day of the murder Glendon arrived on the doorstep out of the blue-he'd come on the train because his bike was in the garage being fixed. Anyway it was a lovely surprise because I really *hadn't* seen him since Christmas. Well we had a chat, something to eat-that sort of thing-but all the while it was like he had something on his mind. That's when he said it-he took my hands in his and said....", she paused, "....that he was about to do something that 'he thought would make me proud. I *am* proud of you I told him-But no, he said, this was something he'd been planning for a while but just wanted to see his 'ol' Mum 'before he went through with it. "

"And what happened then-did he tell you his plans?", Beth asked , hanging onto every word.

"No-just asked if he could borrow a car and that he"d have it back to me soon. Oh Beth I'm worried sick."

She started to cry and Beth walked to the bar and poured her a small brandy.

"Here-drink this", she said sitting down next to her on the lounge.

"Thankyou love. "

Lil took a sip and continued her story. "Well, the car was here the next morning but no Glendon. "

" And are you saying you haven't seen him since?"

"That's right but this was in the car. "

She handed Beth a small piece of paper with a message that read: MUM,

I LOVE YOU-DON'T WORRY-I'M ALRIGHT
WILL CONTACT YOU SOON
GLENDON.

"Beth I wanted to tell you all of this before but I didn't know if I could trust you-you understand I hope?-but now I'm frantic and I didn't know where else to turn. "

"It's alright Lil I understand that but if you really want me to help you, then you must promise to call me as soon as you hear from him-okay?"

She wrote down her hotel address and phone number and placed it in Lil's hand , giving it a slight squeeze in comfort as she did.

"I promise Pet and thankyou-you've been so understanding. "

Beth stayed with her new friend for another hour before deciding it was time to go. "Will you be okay?", she asked. "Yes Love-go on now. "

"Poor thing", Beth said to herself as she drove down the path. She was pleased that Lil never knew had to know that she had actually intended questioning *her* in relation to the murder. Now she knew it was Glendon who had been driving the 'rolls', she must find out more about him. She couldn't really afford to let herself jump to conclusions-especially with Lenny Hill still in the picture-however things were beginning to look fairly obvious. She found herself stopping at a signpost, turning right and heading on in the direction of Chipwick-on-Hemming to pay another visit to P. C. Nancy Briers.

"Hello Beth-welcome back!", said Nancy smiling.

She introduced Beth to the two other officers in the station and added

"See-when somebody experiences one of my special village tours, they just can't keep away! What can we do for you Beth?" "Well I was back in the area and came to see if I could buy a drink-just to say thanks for showing me around last time . "

"Oh that sounds lovely. I'm actually off in ten minutes", she said looking at her watch, "but if they think they can hold the fort without me? ", she added with a smile.....

"Oh get going", laughed one of the officers, "I think we can cope!" "Ooh does this mean I get to ride in the famous Karmann Ghia?", Nancy asked. "Ha! I guess so! Now-which way? You'd know the best places around here. "

Nancy directed Beth to the 'Jolly Abbot'-a small and very welcoming inn on the outskirts of town. They opted for an outside table and took in the chilly country air. "So are you in England for much longer Beth?", Nancy asked. "As long as it takes to free my client." "And how is that coming along?" "Quite good. I've just received some interesting information. Actually Nancy-I was going to ask for a favour "

"Aha-they always say there's no such thing as a free lunch *or* drink!", Nancy joked, "of course I'll help if I can Beth-fire away!"

"Thanks-well I was only going to ask you if knew anything about Glendon Sutton-he's Lil and Frederick Sutton's son. Apparently he's living up north at the moment. "

"Yes I've heard of him of course-Mrs. Sutton is a well known figure around these parts-but I'm afraid I've not been stationed here long enough to know anything about the son. " She paused to think....

"Tell you what though. . I'll bet Anthony would be able to tell you more-or even better still, Neil Jones-remember P. C. Jones?", she added. "Anthony's out of town till tomorrow, but I could let you know then-he's due back early. "

"Oh that would be just great , you're a doll thanks so much. "

"How's your drink?", asked Nancy.

"Gone",

"Another"?

"I think you could twist my arm!"

"Nancy let me ask you something", she added slowly....what do you associate with crematoriums?" "The burning of bodies-why?" "Mm", Beth replied with a shudder. *"Now* you've lost me. ", said Nancy.

Beth quickly explained the existence of the green notebook and one of the numbers in the book being that of 'Redlands Crematorium'.

"As a matter of fact I've been a bit hesitant in facing the whole business-the potential findings are a bit off puting-if you know what I mean!"

"Ooh yes I do", said Nancy pulling a face. But if it's one of your leads then you're going to have to follow it up. 'Redlands' you say?" "Yes that's right. "

"Well come on then, back to the station-I've a couple of good friends back in London. I'll give Jason a ring-he's stationed at Bowdenfield;that way you won't have to ask for any favours at Milton Street-I know some of the attitudes towards P. I. 's!"

They arrived back at the station and Nancy immediately made the call. Beth waited outside taking in the colours and inhaling as much country air as she could before having to return to smoggy old San Paledino!

"Well that's that , no problem there. Jason was only too happy to help-we trained together you know. He's going to get together a list of employees at 'Redlands' and run a check to see if there are any criminal records amongst them-not that that necessarily means anything but it's always a good place to start." "Nancy I really appreciate this-thankyou so much." "Not at all Beth-most exciting thing I've had to do in six months!!", she laughed. "Anyway Jason will have that done tomorrow and he'll let me know, so if I can have your contact number I'll ring you as soon as I hear. "

"Absolutely wonderful-thanks again Nancy. ", Beth said sincerely. scribbling down her address and phone number. "Here -it's the Longmoor Hotel. "

"I'll ask Anthony about the other matter too!", Nancy called as she waved from the steps of the station.

Beth was feeling quite pleased with the day as she drove back into the city. lt was pleasant weather, Nancy had been most helpful and the pub was extra nice! Hopefully, her thoughts continued, she would have some news tomorrow and who knows, with a bit of luck there may even be a message from Lil awaiting her at the 'Longmoor'.

There *was* no message but Beth wasn't too concerned. She read for an hour but felt couped up-all that time in the country had reminded her that there was more to life than small hotel rooms in big noisy cities. She watched the streets below her for a while then tried to read again-but somehow just wasn't able to concentrate. So she donned her favourite new jacket (Sutton's note book securely in top pocket) and was off for a wander. She spotted a little cafe a few days before that she had thought she might like to try so tonight might just be the night.

She walked around for half an hour enjoying the city sights but when the 'grumbles' started up again, it was time to find that 'caf'!! Surprising herself at actually finding something she'd only seen once before, (Beth wasn't known for her great sense of direction!)she proudly headed across the road. But deep in thought about what she felt like eating, Beth was suddenly yanked by her right arm off the street and shoved violently into a poorly lit alley!Thinking quickly, she ran about ten paces to the end-not to try to escape but to be nearer to the only potential weapon she could spot-a row of metal garbage bins. She stood with her back to the wall awaiting the confrontation. Focusing on the figure approaching, it didn't take long for her to realise who it was she was about to be dealing with. This was no random street thug-no random attack. The white suit, the silk tie and handkerchief-only one person would be throwing someone around a dark alley dressed like this.

"Mr. Hill I presume. "

"That's right Darling'-but you can call me Lenny. He came closer toward her and Beth continued to look him straight in the eyes.

"I hear you've been asking a lot of questions about me....must be pretty interested eh?"

"In-your-dreams", she replied slowly and clearly, "now-get-out-of-my-way. "

"Ooh fiery little thing aren't we well as it happens darling. . that's just the way I like it. "

Then, in what seemed like a flash, he'd pulled a knife from his pocket and had flicked the blade to within inches of Beth's face. She remained perfectly still.

"Well well ", he predictably snarled, " not so much to say now eh,

Sweetheart? Right-small talk over-you've got something I want and I intend to have it because what Lenny wants, Lenny always gets. "

Beth swallowed hard. "top left pocket", she said slowly.

It didn't matter that he took it now as she had memorised the important numbers-and besides, she wasn't about to argue with a blade that long.

"I think you've got your wires crossed, Sweet thing I don't give a toss what you got in your pocket", he laughed before his face turned from smug to pure evil. He grabbed her throat tightly.

"It's *you* I want-and you're not gonna try and run are ya' baby 'cause that would make Lenny *very very* mad", he said moving the front of her hair with the knife. " and don't even think about screaming. ", he added with stone cold eyes.

Beth reached slowly and calmly beside her-she realised she had nothing to lose.

"It's your lucky night, bitch, he whispered in her ear", undoing the top button of her blouse ...and you are NEVER going to forget *me*. "

"Nor you , I , Lenny", she replied calmly with a swift knee to the groin. The alley then echoed with the almighty 'clang!' that followed as she brought a 1965 issue metal garbage bin lid crashing down onto his head.

He was instantly on the ground-dazed....shaking his head as if trying to wake from a deep sleep. Kicking the contents of the bin all over him and his now not so white shirt, she quickly grabbed his knife and ran for the lights of the street. Turning to see him holding his head surrounded by the garbage, she glared at him until his eyes met hers. "Consider yourself lucky Mr Hill!" she shouted in a tone seldom heard from Beth's mouth ...and one that made an already shaken Lenny Hill physically shudder.

CHAPTER TWELVE.

Beth was angry. She'd been pulled and shoved, bruised and shaken-and *now* she'd she'd missed her dinner. She kicked the divan in her hotel room in frustration then sat down on the armrest. "Relax old girl", she said to herself, letting out a long breath, "getting all worked up isn't going to help. "

She paced the room for a while then flopped onto her bed. She hadn't thought she was tired but before too long had fallen into a deep sleep-one she'd obviously needed for a while. Startled by a loud ringing at 9 a.m, she shook her head, rubbed her eyes and reached quickly for the phone.

"H-hello?", she answered clearing her throat.
"Beth? It's Nancy Briers-did I wake you?"

Beth filled Nancy in on the previous night's events and Nancy was livid. "You've reported it I assume?"

"I haven't had time-I rushed right home and fell virtually straight to sleep. But yes I *will* report him of course-I'm not going to allow him to try that on anybody else. "

"Good let's see assault and possession of a deadly weapon sounds good for starters-you *can* be in London to testify?"

"Absolutely", said Beth, "whenever I' m required. "

"Bastard", added Nancy.

"I gave him a good hiding", Beth added proudly.

"Well good for you!", said Nancy laughing, "just as long as you're alright. "

"I'm fine-just very angry. "

"And so you should be! Well look, the reason I rang is that first of all, Anthony's back and he's managed to get *some* information on Glendon Sutton for you-now It's not a great deal, but it may help. Anyway I'll just read what he's given me. Okay, apparently he's had more than his fair share of 'run-ins' with the Police;used to ride with a motorbike gang called the 'Ruler's';name's popped up in a few pub brawls;two counts of shoplifting-goods worth total of eighty three pounds. That was four years ago. After that it seems his mother set him up in a shop up North-wanted to get him away from 'bad' influences'! Ah now this bit's interesting-before all of this he had spent some time at a boarding school in Scotland before being expelled for breaking a classmate's nose and from then on", she said with a laugh, Lil had him tutored from home! And that is about all I can tell you I'm afraid. "

"Well that broken nose incident is of interest-a definite violent streak then.

"Yes and also not much joy on the crematorium front either I'm sorry to say. Jason ran a check on all current employees at 'Redlands' and there were no criminal records. Well....", she laughed, "one fellow *had* been arrested last new years eve for urinating in a public place-but I hardly think that links one with the underworld!" "No, I doubt he's our man", laughed Beth. "But what about the owner-anything there?"

"A Mr. William . J. Wilmott and no, nothing-sixty years old, squeaky clean family man by all accounts-but of course one can never be really sure. However I guess that's where your job begins-see what else you can dig up!. "

"Oh look you've all been so helpful-I can't thank you enough and I'll keep Mr. Wilmott in mind-as you say one never really knows." "Any time Beth, it's a pleasure-oh and by the way, Anthony was very jealous of my ride in your car!" "Good to hear!", laughed Beth in reply. "Bye then Beth-call up again." "Bye Nancy-and thanks!"

Well, she thought placing down the phone...our Glendon Sutton sounds as if he could be one very angry young man.

" Something he'd been planning for a while ", she said aloud, remembering his mother's words. "Did you kill your father Glendon? Was it finally payback time??"

Due to the lack of dinner the night before, Beth was now very hungry and so after a visit to the Station to make her report on Lenny Hill, decided to finally try out that cafe. After scrambled eggs and a super-strong espresso she may her way back to the Longmoor.

"Message for you Miss Wade-Beechly!", a voice called from the desk.

"Oh thankyou", said Beth reading the hand written note

BETH,

IMPORTANT NEWS, LUNCH TODAY-12 NOON?

BILLINGTON'S

LIL SUTTON.

"Billington's!", Beth said to herself, "Very fancy."

She returned to her room to ponder what this important news might be.

Noon came around quickly and after a hectic 'why didn't I just get a taxi' kind of drive around the city, Beth finally zoomed Carmen into a space outside the front of Billington's which had just unbelievably become free. She was locking her up when suddenly a heavy hand came down hard on her shoulder. She jumped and turned sharply, looking into the stony eyes that were staring down at her.

He threw his cigarette butt to the ground and stamped it out with a giant black boot.

"Beth Wade-Beechly?" "Yes. ", she replied firmly.

He grabbed her hand and shook it until she thought it could possibly fall off!

"I'm Glendon-Glendon Sutton!", he said, his face bursting into a broad smile. "Oh", said Beth with a sigh of relief, "hello Glendon!"

"Mum sent me out to fetch you . Her and Peggy are inside. . if you'd like to come this way...."

So this was 'little Glendon', she thought to herself with a smile. He was easily six feet five inches tall, was totally clad in black leather, wore a full faced beard and was sporting three very prominent skull rings on each hand. On entering the restaurant Beth spotted Lil and whom she could only assume to be Peggy at a window table on the far side of the room. "Come on then Beth-I want you to meet someone.", Glendon said as he whisked her towards them.

"Hello Lil-I must say you're looking a lot happier that you were the last time we met. "

"Hello Beth, I am indeed....and have I got a story for you! Sit down and have some champagne my love!"

"Champagne?", asked Beth intrigued, " and why do I get the feeling we're celebrating??"

"Because that's exactly what we're doing aren't we my sweet?", said Glendon to the young girl kissing her on the cheek. "Beth I'd like you to meet Peggy my wife. "

"Wife?!", asked Beth slightly amused by the whole scene! "Yes Love-that's the good news. ", said Lil, all smiles. "Here...", she continued, pouring Beth a glass of bubbly, "...get this into you and I'll tell you the whole story. "

She took a sip from her own glass and began .

"When Glendon came to me that night he had something on his mind alright-that sweet little thing sitting next to him-that's what!. . 'some thing that would make me proud' remember? something he'd been planning for a while'??"

"Mm?", said Beth nodding as if waiting for the punchline to a joke. "Well he's only run off and got himself hitched hasn't he?! That's what he was talking about all along the Cheeky little rascal!", she added slapping the back of his head. "These two 'lovebirds' have been up on some Welsh mountain-side honeymooning-if you please-while I've been back 'ere worried sick no doubt about 'em!!"

"Yeah I didn't even know me' Dad got done in", continued Glendon lighting up a cigarette, "see, we had no paper, no radio or anything-just each other", he said gazing into Peggy's eyes. "I went to see him that day too changed my mind the last second. I borrowed Mum's car, parked near his fancy shop. . even walked up to the door. Well then as I said I had second thoughts-always ends up in a fight-and I'm a new man now Beth straight down the line. "

"So you didn't see him at all?", asked Beth.

"No I didn't think it was worth it so I went for a walk instead...and look what I got "

He proudly lowered his jacket to the elbow and lifted the sleeve of his tee shirt to reveal a tattoo of the words....'Peggy forever'.

"Ain't that just dead sweet Beth?" "Oh-oh, yes it's lovely. ", Beth replied to Peggy's first words of the day.

She'd been wondering when Peggy would actually get a word in-and between her new husband and Mother In Law, Beth wondered whether she ever would again!

"So any way", continued 'little' Glendon, "I drove quiet as I could into Mum's house, left the car and took off. If I'd known me' Dad was killed I wouldn't have let her worry like that-we would have come straight back-or at least found a phone to let her know we were okay, wouldn't we Love?", he said turning to his new wife. "Oh yes Mum", Peggy answered.

"Mum!-You hear that Beth?-I've got a new daughter!", Lil said starting to cry.

"Oh come on now Mum, enough of that". laughed Glendon giving Peggy a wink.

"So", he continued, " you found the murderer yet Beth?"

"No Glendon-not yet. "

"Well when you do. you let me know who the bastard is "

The whole table quietened

" I wanna shake his hand!!"

A roar of laughter came from the three of them! Beth too found herself with the giggles-a combination of the whole crazy situation-and of half a glass of champagne!

Another cork was popped, the jokes became progressively louder and Peggy even managed to get two or three more sentences in! It was an enjoyable afternoon but after an extremely over priced and non filling meal and more than just a few condescending looks from the Maitre d', Beth emptied her glass and said her goodbye's. She couldn't have been more pleased to be leaving Lil in such a happy state. Glendon stood and walked her to door.

Thanks for looking after me 'ol Mum. She says you were there for her when she really needed someone-breaks my heart to think of her back here worrying. I think things are starting to work out for us now though. Anyway there's a little present back at your hotel from me and Peggy just to say, well you know, thanks." "Glendon that wasn't necessary-your Mother's a lovely woman-it was my pleasure", she replied.

"Well thanks anyway and goodbye, "he said, giving her another 'handshake from Hell!

Back at the hotel's reception desk, Beth's present was waiting. She *was* a little apprehensive , bringing back to mind Glendon's unique taste in jewellery, but was pleasantly surprised at the sight of two dozen long stemmed pink roses and an enormous box of Swiss chocolates! She smiled from ear to ear- roses had always been her favourite. Taking them to her room, she arranged them in two empty milk bottles, flopped onto the divan and turned on the radio. Putting her feet up, she opened the chocolates, made her selection and to the sounds of Herman's Hermits, happily bit into an almond whirl-her faith in Human nature temporarily restored!

CHAPTER THIRTEEN.

Totally satisfied that Lil and Glendon were off the hook, Beth slept well that night . The morning looked to be the start of a lovely spring day so she decided once again to take herself out to breakfast. She smiled to herself as she found a vacant table imagining the reaction if Bev knew she'd eaten two breakfasts in a row at the *same* cafe! "She'd be *most* insulted!", she said softly whilst studying the menu. Over coffee and an apricot pastry, she pondered her next move- where to go from here. She had to admit that this crematorium business was eating at her. Knowing that Lil and Glendon were innocent had made her happy but unfortunately had also put her right back where she'd started. Susan was still being held for the murder and time was ticking away. Sergeant Brown was more than just a little determined to see her convicted. "Redlands", she said softly, "How are you connected to all of this?"

She took out the green notebook and stared again at the number, then three pages back to Lenny Hill. Suddenly on closer examination she discovered something she had totally overlooked before. "What do we have here?"Next to Hill's name was his contact number and under that, a post box number which she had assumed to be his as well but just now had realized that it was written in a slightly different coloured ink-as if possibly written on a different day. "I just wonder", she said in a whisper.

She finished off her breakfast, put the notebook in her pocket and hurried back to the Longmoor to pick up Carmen. The post box was in the inner city suburb of Bently so was to be quickly and easily found. Growing up in London, Beth knew her way around these parts well and even though most of the buildings had changed, the layout of the streets and suburbs had basically remained the same.

Parking Carmen, she went to the appropriate section of the Bently Post Office.

"117 ", she said quietly, her eyes scanning the rows of numbered boxes, " 117!-Here we are. "

She returned to the car and drove slightly around the corner-enough to still be able to see-but without being obvious. For a moment she wondered what on earth she was doing-this was a long shot to say the least-but what else was left? So she resigned herself to an afternoon of waiting and watching. Her thoughts returned to Lenny Hill and she shook her head in anger. *He* certainly wouldn't be showing up - even if it were his post box-the Police would have picked him up by now.

"Bastard", she said under her breath.

If it did belong to somebody else or perhaps somebody working for Hill, then she desperately hoped they might show up today. But nobody did- and four hours later Beth gave up.

She felt down...in a rut. The weather had turned cold and it was starting to rain. After picking up some dinner on the way home, she also bought a bottle of wine. Things weren't falling into placed like she had hoped. She thought she'd found the murderer in Glendon Sutton and now that he was cleared, it was like starting all over again.

"Well, as they say in the movies ", she said opening the bottle, " tomorrow *is* another day. "

Beth had never been a big drinker and so with each glass of wine her thoughts of the case drifted further and further from her mind and by the time poured the last few drops, she was well and truly contemplating the great mysteries of her time . . Will there ever be world peace?....is there life on other planets?...how does a vacuum flask keep things both hot AND cold??

Soon after that she was sound asleep on the divan. "Ooooooh", she groaned shading her eyes after being woken up to the morning sun-(any other morning she would have greeted it with a smile). She sat up slowly, rubbed her eyes, and stood up and swayed on the spot.

"Oooooow ", she moaned and held her head, catching a sight of the empty bottle, and feeling more than a little queezy. 'Never again...never *ever* again. " She dragged herself to the sink for a glass of water, groaning with each tentative step.

Funnily enough Beth didn't feel like breakfast that morning but after a chat with Susan at the station, was beginning to crave a strong hot cup of tea. She slowly made her way to the cafeteria to be greeted by a waving P. C. Somersby. She waved back, bought her tea and joined him at his table-hoping that he wasn't going to be in an over talkative mood. (Beth liked Lee Somersby but at this point her head felt near to the point of explosion!) '"Morning

Ma'am", he said chirpily, standing as she approached.

"Good morning Lee how are you today?", She replied, slowly but successfully getting the words out between the throbs.

"Mind if I join you two?", asked a pleasantly (to Beth's current state) soft voice.

"Not at all Sir. "

"Hello David", Beth added yawning and drinking some tea. She screwed up her face at the first mouthful and noticed that both men were looking at her concerned.

"Are you alright Beth?", asked David.

"Yes, yes I'm fine really....just a bit of a....headache, that's all. "

Lee looked down at the table with a half smile while David looked straight at Beth and smiled.

"Yes alright, alright, it's a hangover then I admit it lock me up and throw away the key!"

David laughed, "Say no more-we've all been *there*!" Turning to Lee he added, "P. C. Somersby might be kind enough to rummage up a couple of aspirin. "

"Oh yes of course Sir-won't be long Ma'am" and he was off!

"Thanks David I think that's exactly what I need." "Beth', David said, his smile fading slightly, "I really wanted to speak to you alone-I have to tell you that things aren't looking very positive-for Miss Morris I mean. I *was* hoping you may have something for me. "

Beth frowned and shook her head. "I'm afraid not. I thought I was onto something but no joy. "

"Mm it's just that Richard Brown seems to have a definite bee in his bonnet about this case-really pushing for it to get into court. Anyway I wanted to warn you. "

"Oh speak of the devil", Beth said rolling her eyes after spotting Brown in the distance.

At that point P. C. Somersby arrived back smiling with a cup of water and two white tablets. "Oh thankyou Lee-that's lovely." "My pleasure Ma'am!"

"Now I would *definitely* stay out of his way today Beth , "David warned looking in Brown's direction. He paused and turned to Lee, " well you know the story better than I do constable "

"Yes Sir". replied Lee excitedly, "Well Ma'am last night..... . ", he began as if appearing in court, " P. C. Davis and myself were called to a domestic dispute. Well it happened to be the residence of Sergeant Brown Ma'am. Mrs. Brown had locked him out and was in the process of throwing his clothes and belongings out and onto the street. "

"Really?", said Beth innocently.

"Yes really-calling him all the names under the sun and screaming something about escorts and call girls!.......kept saying that this was the last straw, this was the excuse she'd been looking for and that kind of thing. It was quite a sight Ma'am , as you could imagine!"

"And of course by now it's all around the station", David added. 'I shouldn't laugh really-but I will!"

"Well Goodness Me that's quite a story-I wonder what could have happened", Beth said smiling.

And suddenly her headache was gone!

Lee stood to return to work and nodding at Beth said "Nice to see you again Ma'am-and I hope you're feeling better soon. "

David also had to leave and so said goodbye to Beth. After a few paces though, he stopped and turned back.

"Beth?", he asked quizically, " is it my imagination or does Lee Somersby become extremely what's the word efficient in your presence?- Ma'am this, Ma'am that?"

"Um-er-no it's not your imagination David", she replied slowly and with a grin, "let's just say it's a very long and slightly-just slightly, mind-dishonest story!"

"Oh I see", said David nodding with smile, "Private Detective tactics eh?"

"Er-something like that. "

"I won't ask!", he laughed, "Bye Beth. "

Alone at the table Beth's smile faded. David's words repeated in her mind but he hadn't told her anything she didn't already know-time *was* ticking away. She must get things together and quickly-she had a young woman's life to save.

It was still early and although her headache had ceased, Beth's body was dragging. It wasn't about to let her forget the way she had abused it the night before. She decided to drive home via the Post Office and hope for something to break-it had to be worth another try.

She parked Carmen in the same place and with camera in hand began watching and waiting....and waiting....and waiting-nothing. Two long hours had passed and deciding to give it ten more minutes, her spirits were suddenly lifted when a taxi pulled up directly in front of the post box section. She reached for her camera and peered through it ready to start snapping. A figure left the car, ran straight to box 117 and looking around nervously, unlocked the box, removed an envelope, locked the box again and ran back to the waiting taxi.

The drizzle was turning to rain and photographs would have been quite unclear. But Beth wouldn't be needing any pictures;she wouldn't forget the face. The camera dropped to her lap and her heart sank. "Bevan....", she said softly, "....Bevan Scott."

CHAPTER FOURTEEN.

That night Beth's head was in a spin.

"Bevan Hill Redlands. " She repeated the words over and over.

"There's something missing. "

She drew up a page with three columns and under each heading added all of the facts she'd gathered on each. Was there a connection? Was one party responsible for Sutton's death? Where they in cahoots?Or was it somebody entirely different?... somebody unknown to everybody?

Putting it to one side, she felt almost totally disparaged and so reached for that day's newspaper-flicking through it but without really taking anything in. "Australian woman scoops lottery jackpot....well good for you! ", she said reading on. "Thirty seven year old nurse from Victoria...well done, you!

Beth's thoughts of the case wouldn't allow her to concentrate on anything else and so after rolling her eyes at the social pages, she put the paper aside as well. She walked slowly across the room to the window for some air. The cold night air stung her face but she hardly noticed-thoughts and ideas still repeated in her mind.

"I need a talk with Gran maybe I'm looking too hard maybe I'm looking in the wrong direction. "

Either way, one thing was for certain-a visit with Selina *always* lifted her spirits one hundred percent. In fact she almost immediately started to feel happier and suddenly becoming aware of the cold London air , reached for her jacket as she prepared to return to the future-only to realize she'd left it in the car! "Damn!", she yelled as a wave of panic and self anger tore through her body.

"The book!", she added, "Sutton's note book. how could I have been so thoughtless?!"

Rushing to the elevator and out onto the street she soon saw she was too late. The car had been broken into , the jacket hanging halfway out the door. She grabbed it and felt for the note book.

"Gone", she said walking to the front of Carmen and sitting on her bonnet.

At this stage the notebook itself wasn't as important as who would want to take it. "Damn!", she said again, kicking an empty can into the gutter.

Letting out a long slow sigh she retrieved the can, patted the car on the roof, slowly put on her jacket and wandered disheartenedly back inside.

"Where to now old girl?, she asked herself lying once again on the divan. Holding the Christmas party photograph in her hands. She said aloud

"Who killed you Frederick Sutton?"

Her thoughts turned to Susan. Reality hit her hard as she realized that this young woman could go to prison for life if she didn't do something soon. Staring desperately at the photograph she she said once again..."*Who* killed you?"

Suddenly she sprang to her feet.

"Hold on a second ...that newspaper?!. . ", she said flicking frantically through the pages, "here ...Lottery numbers numbers NUMBERS! Of course....that's it!!"

She dropped the paper onto the coffee table and went to the window in a half dazed state.

"Oh yes of course", she beamed pacing back across the floor and grabbing the Christmas picture once again. "Beth old girl-how could you have been so slow?!"

She held it in front of her and slowly nodded, "So...it *was* you it *was* you afterall. "

Quickly phoning the Police, Beth raced outside and jumped into her trusty Carmen. "I just hope I'm not too late!"

It was only a matter of minutes before Beth arrived at Sutton's office, quietly making her way in and taking her position. "Thank goodness", she whispered to herself, "looks like I made it first. "

Approximately forty minutes had passed but Beth wasn't concerned-this time she *knew* she wasn't wrong.

Suddenly the door to the office opened and she watched as a figure in the familiar black outfit walked straight to the wall safe (hidden behind a painting) opened the door and lifted out a small suitcase. Closing the door carefully and turning to leave the office, the figure was suddenly stunned by the bright flash of Beth's torch. She immediately she switched on the main lights to the office.

"Doing a spot of overtime..... . Detective Brody?

No need to tell me what's in the case", she said calmly, "I think I can guess. "

He said nothing-just stared emotionless. But it's what she had expected-he was good, too good to ever speak without thinking about what he was going to say.

"In fact, "Beth continued confidently , "let me tell you *my* scenario and we'll see how close I am. "

"I'm intrigued Beth", was his smooth reply, "please go on." "You were Sutton's 'plant' at Milton Street Station. I'd suspected there was a bent copper in the midst the day you yourself told me about Brown's bungled stake out-but until now I wasn't totally sure who it was. You either wanted 'out' or you wanted a payrise-I'd personally bet on the latter-but Sutton wouldn't agree *and* wouldn't let you go. In fact I think he threatened you-get on with your job or you'd be exposed...something like that? He probably told you he had material or evidence on you locked away somewhere safely . Well it doesn't take one long to deduct where such documents would be kept-especially for a man of your Policing skills. " 'I'm flattered Beth-please continue. "

"I think you came here on the evening of the murder to try to find the combination of the safe. You thought you'd be alone-the store being closed, you didn't count on Sutton having not one but two guests. You hid when you heard him return and decided to wait it out. You would have seen Theresa Scott come and go then not long after that, Susan Morris. You saw what went on and no doubt the anger in Susan's eyes when she stabbed the desk-but that wasn't all you saw-you also spotted the infamous green notebook and realised that it most probably contained what you were looking for-the combination for Sutton's safe. It was then you had the idea to murder Frederick Sutton. How easy-Susan would surely be blamed. Then all you had to do was get the book and retrieve the suitcase . And so , as you watched Sutton go to lock the doors after Susan had left, you grabbed the letter opener from the desk hoping (rightly I presume) that Sutton would be too drunk to notice it gone. You waited until he had sat down again and that's when you made your move. All that was left then was the notebook-that was you I saw at Susan's apartment and you who grabbed me at my hotel. But you didn't get the book until tonight and I knew you wouldn't waste much time picking up that suitcase containing all of that lovely incriminating evidence-a veritable 'case of crime'.

She paused then gave a short laugh through her nose.

"You know it wasn't until a newspaper article brought my attention to numbers that I realized what was going on. I had the combination all along but I assumed it to be a phone number. You see it just also happened to be the phone number of a local crematorium and *that's* what threw me. But then it hit me and as soon as I opened my mind to the limitless possibilities that a series of numbers could represent, it quickly fell into place-a safe combination. "

She paused once again for the finale...*this* , she was going to enjoy.

"But you know what gave you away in the end Inspector? "oh do tell Beth", was his patronising tone, "you haven't disappointed so far". "It was your greed, sir-plain and simply your Greed. - oh and your weakness for accessories. You stole from a dead man . . like a common little criminal.

His sarcastic smile dropped as he realised to what she must have been refering.

"The very first day I met you I couldn't help noticing the most attractive and unusual tie pin you were wearing-the same one Frederick Sutton was wearing at a Christmas party just three months before. I've never seen it on you since';you obviously realised your mistake quickly enough. Luckily for you , Susan Morris was far too upset that day to notice it nor recognise it. But you didn't count on the existence of a certain photograph-sometimes dead men *do* tell tales. I'm sure your most efficient Police Force will easily find the evidence in question at your home. Just couldn't help yourself could you?-just had to have that little bit extra. Well that's *my* version", she ended, "how did I do?"

He smiled dryly and gave two short laughs.

"Very good Beth I'm most impressed-a most intriguing tale . . and such a shame they'll be the last words you will ever speak. What?...", he added, " no cavalry?", he asked looking sarcastically around the room. "And don't expect them to show either-not after the file I put together on you. I'm Sorry Beth but a man has to cover his tracks-you know how it is. "

He pulled a gun slowly from his pocket and pointed it at her. "Not a very sensible idea with two officers standing behind you", she said.

"Oh please Beth", he replied almost sympathetically, "if you think I'm going to fall for that old chestnut you really have been playing detective too long. "

He raised the gun "Goodbye Beth Wade-Beechly-until we meet again..."

"I'll take that Sir!", came the ever efficient voice of P. C. Somersby, "there's more than one hiding place in this office you know. "

Lee handcuffed a stunned Brody as P. C. Davis took the suitcase. "Well done boys!" said Beth. "Wait...just one more thing", she added turning to a now furious looking Detective, "you were watching as Sutton attacked Theresa Scott. What if he hadn't have stopped? What if he had gone further-would you have stepped in?"

His silence answered the question. "Just as I thought ", Beth nodded as she looked him up and down, " you're an evil bastard, David Brody. "

"For once I agree with you Sweetheart", said D. S. Brown appearing from nowhere and throwing a punch directly into Brody's mouth. "Nothin' worse than a crooked cop-I've 'ad my eye on you for a while Brody", he added being held back by P. C. Davis.

They led the assailant out toward a waiting car and Brown turned at the door. " and as for you ya smart-mouthed little trouble maker, I think now would be a good time for you to get out of town...and stay out!"

Beth couldn't be bothered replying. Instead, now alone in the office she sat down at the desk, relaxed her body, let out a long breath-and smiled.

'It's over", she said, "it's over. "

CHAPTER FIFTEEN.

Beth was up bright and early in the morning feeling very pleased with herself indeed. She started the day with a walk in the park stopping on the way for a loaf of bread to feed the pigeons. On her return to the Longmoor, she was met in the foyer by an exhuberant Susan Morris.

"Beth!", she said throwing her arms around her. 'Thankyou so much-I don't know what I can ever do to repay you-I owe you my life!" "Oh yes you really do don't you?!", Beth replied jokingly. "Susan it was my absolute pleasure. I'm just so happy everything has worked out the way it has. "

Susan paused.

"Theresa told me what happened with Freddy. Thanks for not telling me-it would have really upset me back then but....", she shook her head slowly, ". . I'm beginning to realise he really *wasn't* the man I thought he was. Anyway I'm not going to dwell on the past...you've that you've given me back my future and *that's* what im going to focus on!. Now I certainly hope you've nothing planned for this evening. "

"No I haven't-why?"

"Good! Because you're coming to a party at Bevan and Theresa's. It's their twentieth wedding anniversary -and it's also to celebrate my release!"

"Oh that sounds wonderful!", said Beth.

"Terrific!-eight o'clock then? I must go-lots of organising to do!!"

Susan smiled "Thankyou again Beth Wade-Beechly" she said, kissing her on the cheek.

She ran off excitedly down the road leaving Beth to her thoughts.

"Oh Beth!", Susan called from a little way off, "these are for you-a promise is a promise!", she added hurling a half empty packet of cigarettes through the air.

"Good girl!", called Beth in reply catching them in one hand and tossing them into the nearest bin.

Beth was car-less today and so decided to do something outrageously touristy-she took a bus tour of the city! Carmen was with P. C. Davis who had kindly offered to fix her door after the break in the night before. From the top of a double decker bus Beth's thoughts continued. She still had the problem of Bevan . How ever was he connected to Sutton and how on earth was she going to approach it?

Eight o'clock soon came around and after picking up Carmen, some wine and some chocolates , Beth once again arrived at the Scott's warm and welcoming home. Susan was there along with Theresa, Bevan, Marjorie Burgess and little Katrina.

"Come on in Beth-P. I. extraordinaire!!". called Bevan with obviously one or two drinks already under his belt. "We all owe you so much Beth", he added.

"Alright then pass me over one of those ales and we'll call it even!"

"Whoah-ho! That's the girl!", he laughed.

Theresa smiled and gave Beth a kiss. "Susan's told you it's our twentieth today?"

"Yes Theresa congratulations-oh these are for you-sorry they're not wrapped." "Oh Bevan look what Beth's brought us, how lovely. "

"Oooh thankyou Beth this looks a good drop!", he said reading the label on the bottle of wine.

"Yes well not tonight!", Theresa laughed snatching it back from him. "Speaking of presents", said Susan, "show Beth yours Theresa." "Ooh yes do", Beth said curiously.

Theresa proudly held out her hand to show a beautifully set gold and ruby ring.

"Sneaky thing I've *always* wanted a ruby ring and I didn't suspect a thing, not a thing", Theresa explained, "not even Susan knew about it-then we find out that he purposely kept it from her in case she gossiped to me!"

"Yes, gossip! Me! There's not enough time to gossip working for that slave driver!"

"I'll second that!", said Marjorie.

"Huh! Rubbish!", Bevan shouted with a grin, "You do your fair share Marjorie Burgess!!"

"Tell Beth how you pulled it off Love", Theresa said turning to her husband.

"Well I'd asked Sutton to make me up a ring-something a bit different. I had a rough idea in my mind which I jotted down. Then he was to make it up for me going on what I'd drawn. But try...", he laughed, glancing cheekily at Susan and Theresa, "...keeping anything from these two! So anyway it was like real spy stuff Beth. Sutton opened a post office box and gave me a key. The plan was that when the ring was ready he could put it there where I could leave the money when I picked it up. Well with all the confusion of everything that happened I forgot to check the post office box until yesterday and sure enough-the ring was there. "

"Ooh very 007!", laughed Beth. "But Bevan....", she asked, "....you were hardly what I would have called Sutton's biggest fan. . so why on earth give *him* the business? Surely there are plenty of other jewellers in town. "

"Er well....", said Bevan blushing, "I er...."

"Yes", said Theresa, "I hadn't thought of that. "

"Oh I think I can answer *that* one!", laughed Marjorie knowingly who was warming herself by the fireplace, "I *did* grow up with him you know. Now how shall I put this? You see Bevan was always the boy who ran a lemonade stall in the summer holidays."

The three women looked at her with rather puzzled expressions.

"Let's just say that if there was a 'bob' to be made or to be *saved* then Bevan was definitely your boy. "

Beth smiled at Susan with Theresa catching on a moment later. "Ooh you rotten cheapskate!", Theresa said hitting him with a sofa cushion, " he offered you a discount didn't he?!"

"One I couldn't refuse!!", Bevan replied with a roar of laughter.

Beth joined in the laughter and then added..... "but if you picked up the ring...."

"That's right!", said Bevan, "we never actually paid for it! So as soon as I picked it up I went straight to the nearest travel agency and booked us a week's holiday to sunny Spain!"

"We're off on a second honeymoon Beth", Theresa said smiling.

"Cheapskate!", she added hitting him once more with the cushion.

"Oh and by the way Beth Bevan knows about the loan, I couldn't keep it in any longer-no more secrets ever again.

A happy ending then, Beth thought to herself. How relieved she was to know that this was Bevan's only connection to Frederick Sutton. She had hated ever doubting either of them ...but, her thoughts continued ...once a detective always a detective!

Theresa excused herself to answer the phone while Beth chatted to Marjorie. It turned out she'd grown up next door to Bevan's family and had remained close friends with him ever since. And as coincidence may have it, she was living only four doors away now.

After a few minutes Theresa returned looking slightly puzzled but at the same time very happy. "Something quite peculiar has just happened-but most exciting!"

She sat down and continued.

"That was Lillian Sutton on the phone just now." "Lillian Sutton?!", said a startled Susan.

"Yes well somehow she's managed to see some of our designs and well get this-she wants to go into business with us! We design and make the clothing and she provides the financial backing. Any way she wants to meet us for lunch tomorrow-at 'Billington's' if you please!-to discuss it!"

"Oh I can't believe it-this is wonderful!", said a beaming Susan. "That *is* wonderful", agreed Beth, "and believe me, if you decide to go through with it, you couldn't find a better-or a nicer business partner."

Bevan raised his glass.

"Well what a night of celebrations! HERE'S CHEERS!"

After a wonderful night Beth said her well wishes and goodbyes and sincerely promised to come back and visit. She had always considered this one of the biggest advantages of time travel- the fact that she could return at any moment...and this was one promise she fully intended to keep!

Beth returned to the 'Longmoor[1] for what was to be her final night. She was going to miss the place that had become her temporary home.

Her last morning had finally arrived and getting her things together, she made a quick phonecall to Nancy to thank her for all she'd done. Nancy informed her that word of Brody had quickly reached Chipwick-on-Hemming and OakWillow and that it was definitely *the* biggest news to hit the towns for years!

She checked out of the hotel, apologising to the divan for the odd angry kick, jumped into Carmen and once again took a long last drive around the 1965 version of the city of London. She was anxious to return to San Paledino but first there were still two young men that she really wanted to see.

Pulling up again at Milton Street Station she put the top on Carmen because although it was dry at that moment, it had rained for most of the night and was again looking decidedly glum. The ground was wet under foot so Beth made her way carefully to the front entrance. She was lucky to catch them as P. C. Somersby and P. C. Davis were just finishing their shift. They were chatting for a few moments on the doorstep when suddenly the door swung open harshly at the hands of Richard Brown, hitting Beth in the arm.

"So sorry Sweetheart-didn't see you there", he said sarcastically, laughing as he stomped off and mumbling "stupid little cow" under his breath.

Lee and Alan looked both disgusted and embarrassed. "Oh Ma'am....I....I", stuttered Lee appearing to be totally lost for words.

"Yes I know Lee....", said Beth, "....but don't worry-I'm a firm believer in Karma." After a quick explanation to Lee on what karma was, Alan nodded, "well he's certainly got a lot of it coming his way-just hope I'm around to see it!", he laughed.

"Yes indeed", agreed Beth and thought how typical it was that Brown had eventually needed to resort to physical violence.

She said her farewells and returned to Carman, looking back toward the building as she started her up. "Bye bye for now Milton Street Station!"

She pulled out from her parking spot and suddenly spotted what appeared to be *the* most unbelievably wonderful opportunity . About twenty metres in front of her was Detective Sergeant Richard Brown shovelling what looked to be an enormous cream cake into his mouth and washing it down with a large bottle of soft drink. He had stopped right next to a giant mud-filled pot hole, filled from the night's rain and was trying to light a cigarette. Beth turned and winked at the waving P. C. Davis, slammed her foot on the excellerator, sped up behind him and screeched to a halt-absolutely covering him in a shower of mud and water! Winding down her window she called "So sorry Sweetheart-didn't see you there!!", and quickly sped off to the applause of some nearby children. She never looked back!

Beth drove for about an hour until she reached a field and parked Carmen near a river and out of sight of the main roads. She kissed her bonnet and smiled. Then with a typically mischievous expression added "..... Don't worry darling-I'll be back before you know it."

Looking around her for one last time she bid farewell to the sixties and slowly closed her eyes.

EPILOGUE.

Beth's bedroom was a welcomed sight. The purple velvet curtains, her paisley print bath robe hanging behind the door-the photos, the lava lamps-even the bookshelf looked like an old friend (although she wished Sarah would stop buying her those tacky women's detective novels-some of them were just *too* far fetched)!

She had the place to herself as, it being a weekday Sarah would have been at the office. She switched on the television and made herself a decaf. The case was solved, Susan was free, Brody was in custody and Brown was covered in mud. She smiled and felt content-but that's not all she felt. A grumbling sound soon reminded her that it was far too long since she'd had some of Beverly's famous mud cake!

"Well you're looking quite pleased with yourself", said Bev smiling warmly as always.

"That I am", replied Beth sitting herself down at her favourite table. "Aah yet another successful case!", she added jokingly. "Well congratulations Lovely lady. . , I'm pleased for you. Cake and coffee on the house then!"

Beth watched her walk toward the kitchen. If there was someone else she'd like to know her secret it was definitely Bev. "Maybe one day", she said quietly to herself...'maybe one day'.

After praising chef-Bev on the 'amazingly joyous experience' of yet another huge piece of cake (they seemed to be getting bigger all the time), Beth reserved her table for lunch the following day.

"By that time I should be hungry again!", she laughed holding her stomach. "Tomorrow then", said Bev, "....and Beth....congratulations again". "

Beth bought some champagne and then rang Selina asking her to meet her at the office-and to bring Mum. The case was closed and they had some celebrating to do!

Selina was delighted and 'ever so proud' of her two 'wonderful Grand Daughters' and before too long Selina, Beth and Sarah were together again in the office. Sarah put the 'office closed' sign on the door while Beth popped the cork on the *first* champagne bottle. Beth thanked Sarah profusely for running things at work while she;d been away after Selina had told her what a marvellous job she'd been doing.

"Yes well just don't forget ", said Sarah studying the label on the bottle, " from now on *you* can handle our Mr. Edwards!

Beth laughed as she ruffled Sarah's hair. "Are you really closed-or are you just trying to keep the likes of me out?!", came Maria's voice from the door. "Mum!", said Beth, "Come in!"

"Got your message ", Maria said to Selina, " I hope there's still some champagne left!"

"Here you are Mum", said Sarah who had as efficiently as ever already poured her a glass.

"Thankyou Darling Oh Sweetheart I thought you might be interested in this", Maria added to Beth handing her a copy of that day's newspaper, folded back and opened at the social pages. "Top left", she said.

"Hmm thanks for the thought Mum but I think you'll find Aunt Dorothy is the Engelbert Humperdinck fan. "

"Oh not that picture you cheeky girl! The one next to it", she laughed.

"Oh!", Beth said with happy surprise.

She read aloud..."Pictured accepting the British Fashion Industry's award for excellence for the third consecutive year is C. E. O of Suresa Fashions, Katrina Scott. "Gosh, how wonderful", Beth beamed.

"Oh she looks lovely", added Sarah peering over Beth's shoulder. "Selina's kept me up to date with the details of the case", explained Maria, "so when I saw this I couldn't wait to show you!"

She paused and smiled.

"Congratulations girls-to 1965!"

"A good year that", laughed Beth. "Actually....", she continued slowly, "...that brings me to something I've been wondering about. "

"I know that tone", Sarah said quickly, "she wants something!"

"Well not so much *wants* something as would like to *keep* something. Now I know I'm not supposed to benefit personally from my time travelling and I know I really shouldn't even be suggesting..."

Her Grandmother nodded.

"What you seem to be having trouble saying Dear, is that you'd like to keep the car. "

All eyes fell on Selina and Sarah sighed. "You know the rules Beth", her grandmother added . "Yes Gran, I suppose I *was* just being selfish. "

"However ", she continued, "....it *is* your birthday soon and if there was a chance that your mother , older sister and myself would be chauffeured into the country for a lovely picnic from time to time..."

"Oh Gran!", beamed Beth, "you mean I can keep her?!"

"Yes darling you can keep her", replied Selina giving Maria a wink.

"Yes well that's all well and good but just don't go reappearing with it down on Main Street or the likes!" added Sarah quickly and predictably.

She continued. . "so-thirty five this year-are you going to do something special?"

"Oh ", Beth replied with 'that' look in her eye," nothing *special* probably just sit around all day relishing in the fact that I'll always be three years younger than you! Ha ha!"

"Beth!", Maria said playfully scolding.

"You see Mum?-you see what I have to put up with?", Sarah said trying to hide her smile. "She's always going on about karma and that sort of thing-well you just wait-one of these days little sister-one of these days!"

Everybody laughed and Selina topped up their glasses. The phone rang and a now slightly tipsy Beth yelled. .

"They'll be lucky! Tell 'em we're closed Sis!"

"Wade-Beechly Investigations?", answered Sarah, successfully disguising a champagne-induced hiccup, "....Oh Mr. Edwards how lovely to hear your voice!. . Beth? Why yes-as a matter of fact she is"!

She swivelled around smugly on her chair and handed Beth the phone. "Karma!", she said with a very large smile indeed!